T0128036

Moore, Than a Pretty Face

Ashlee Wynters

BALBOA
PRESS

A DIVISION OF HAY HOUSE

Balboa Press books may be ordered through booksellers or by contacting:

Balboa Press
A Division of Hay House
1663 Liberty Drive
Bloomington, IN 47403
www.balboapress.com.au
1 (877) 407-4847

Because of the dynamic nature of the Internet, any web addresses or
links contained in this book may have changed since publication and
may no longer be valid. The views expressed in this work are solely those
of the author and do not necessarily reflect the views of the publisher,
and the publisher hereby disclaims any responsibility for them.

The author of this book does not dispense medical advice or prescribe the use
of any technique as a form of treatment for physical, emotional, or medical
problems without the advice of a physician, either directly or indirectly. The
intent of the author is only to offer information of a general nature to help
you in your quest for emotional and spiritual well-being. In the event you use
any of the information in this book for yourself, which is your constitutional
right, the author and the publisher assume no responsibility for your actions.

Any people depicted in stock imagery provided by Getty Images are
models, and such images are being used for illustrative purposes only.
Certain stock imagery © Getty Images.

Print information available on the last page.

ISBN: 978-1-5043-1389-6 (sc)
ISBN: 978-1-5043-1390-2 (e)

Balboa Press rev. date: 07/30/2018

This is for you;

Mum, Rhys and my love Cameron, without you, this would still be a dream

CONTENTS

CHAPTER 1

Ella Jade

EVERY DAY STARTS the same way for me. The alarm sounds at 4:45 a.m., and I get out of bed and help my husband get ready for work, making him his breakfast and lunch. He is not a morning person by any stretch and cannot function in the slightest, so I have always helped him get ready in the morning before sending him on his way. As soon as my husband walks out the door, I throw on my exercise tights and sneakers and run for about five kilometres, from our house to our local general store and back again. I come home and stretch out my body with the flow of yoga, have a shower, get dressed, do my make-up, and then I am off to make my fifty-minute commute to my job. I have pretty much the same day six days a week every week of the year, with Sunday being the only exception, as my husband works every Saturday.

My name is Ella Jade Moore. I'm thirty-one years old, and I am a wife, daughter, sister, and friend. I have always felt like two people. One part of me is an insecure girl who strives to be the perfect wife, lover, and best person she possibly can be. The other part of me is a dark, careless sexually free woman whom

1

I fight to try to keep under control! I know my own insecurity and fears are the reasons I try so hard to be the perfect wife. I grew up with parents in an old-fashioned type of marriage, where my father had full control over the family and money. My mother was a beautiful and kind woman. She was always put together nicely, and her hair and make-up were forever perfect. She was beyond beautiful and caught the eyes of most men wherever she went. She had a body that could make any man weak at the knees and a face that turned heads. She had an incredible brave face, she tolerated a lot from my father, and she was the most forgiving person I have ever known.

Many people never realised the control my father possessed over her. He was an extremely jealous and insecure man, and he knew my mother was out of his league, which is why he always brought her down and made her feel she was worthless, as if she didn't deserve anything better than him. She always stressed about the tidiness of our home. I guess she thought that if she kept the house clean, toys contained, dinner on the table, and coffee ready for when he walked in the door every night, everything would be okay! My father had a deceiving talent for making people believe he was a kind, happy, life-loving family man, which was far from the truth. He always put on a great show in public, so I think it was hard for people to believe otherwise.

I am always trying to justify my actions and thoughts. Whether I blame it on my hormones or my overactive imagination, I am constantly psychoanalysing myself—you know, there has to be a reason why I feel like this today and I didn't yesterday. This is part of the reason I have such a structured lifestyle; it helps keep me in check! The other part is my husband. He loves structure and routine. From the time I rise until the time I fall asleep at night, my day is heavily organised.

I am a gluten-intolerant vegan. My husband is a normal omnivore; he eats anything and everything. For every mealtime, I prepare two separate meals. When I say I'm a vegan, most people roll their eyes at me if to say, *Another tree-hugging, animal-saving hippie.* For me personally, it has never been about saving the world. I am only one person, and I cannot eat dairy, so I found it easier to say vegan, as I am a vegetarian as well. I have always enjoyed eating this way from the time I was a small child. At mealtimes, my mother always put more vegetables on my plate than meat to prevent arguments with my father, as I didn't ever want to eat meat! I never enjoyed the taste, texture, or the heavy feeling in my stomach. I have always found it easier on me to make my food plainer than my husband's, as it is quicker for me to whip up after a long day at work. That's the reason I truly appreciate the food and flavours when I eat out, as I don't get to eat exotic food very often.

I once read that my zodiac sign is very imaginative, that I am a passionate lover who cannot help but try to please. I am fiercely independent and can be reluctant to devote myself 100 per cent to a long-term commitment; however, when I do decide to settle down, it will be with permanence in mind. Money and material possessions are not important to me. While I have always understood that money is a necessity to survive, I don't value it too highly or strive for it. I do like to own nice things but don't feel the need to be surrounded by them. It also read that it was important that I not choose a career that involves going to the same place every day, as life is about the experience, not the big plan.

I tend to agree with this in all aspects of my life. It's truly amazing how just one paragraph can sum up your entire life! I bore easily, have no connection to household possessions, feel that money is a necessity but not something I yearn for, and find my job to be extremely repetitive. Yes, I like a structured lifestyle, but sometimes I find it all too much. You know the old saying "If you build your walls too tight, they might all come crashing down!" I am an accountant at a major Investment Firm, and I work on the seventeenth floor of a twenty-third-storey office building just outside of the city. I have my own office, so it's not as if I am stuck in a booth all day … but I still find myself completely fucking bored 97 per cent of the time. I sometimes spend part of my day ripping strips of paper off my notepad, rolling them up, and then flicking them towards the bin in my office like a child.

I am lucky that my office window has a view of the ocean, but it also has its downfalls. When I am admiring its beauty, I remember that I am locked in a concrete box for the next eight hours and the feeling quickly goes away! I find myself wondering, *Is this really my life, crunching numbers every day for people who don't give a shit because they are all waiting for their long service to kick in or retirement age so they can access their superannuation.* To be honest, I am great at my job. The problem is that I just don't have the passion or truly care for what I do! I feel that my intelligence is wasted, and I spend my time daydreaming and having the people underneath me do all the actual work.

When I was a child, people always made comments to my parents about my looking into the clouds—they used to call me "the flower child." It seemed like to them that I had no cares. My daydreams have always been so creative. My parents had photos of me squatting down on the ground, completely zoned out. I remember that I could sit there for hours, running sand and dirt granules through my fingers, absolutely oblivious of the world around me.

My daydreams are strange thoughts that I try to control, depending on my mood or hormones on how fairy-like or explicit they can become. I tell myself all the time that there has to be something wrong with me! As I sit in traffic on my commute, I sometimes wonder, *Do the people in that car next to me have similar thoughts? Are they happy with their lives?* Sometimes I dream about running away or making a big move, and then sometimes they become more sinister fantasies of my being someone else, being with someone else. It's not necessarily cheating; it's more imagining what it would be like if I were in a different body with a different life with a different man? Would I be truly happy? Would I still be bored? Or would I finally be myself? I find myself standing naked in front of the mirror and looking at myself, just standing there staring at my naked body, the body I wear as a shell, the cover for my soul. I find myself asking, "What is so good about this body I have been given!" as I pinch my skin and watch the girl in the mirror looking back at me in my reflection. I wonder who she really is, who I really am.

When people look at me, within ten seconds, I believe they think they have me all worked out—that they feel they know exactly who I am—and I am judged by that! Older women usually smile and tell me how nice it is to see a young lady making an effort in her appearance, as most don't do that these days. Young to middle-aged women give me filthy death looks. Men look me up and down, sometimes making me feel dirty or even sick, for in that split second, I am able to see into their eyes and get a glimpse of what they would do to me if they ever got me alone.

My mother always told me from the time I was a small girl that being a woman and having female parts automatically puts you at risk in life and that you must always be vigilant. It is so true! Knowledge is power. That is always in the back of my mind, and it has saved me so many times. I don't go anywhere without my pepper spray in my handbag, as I have been stalked numerous times in my life. Some of the men have been previous lovers, and others have been work colleagues or even strangers who have seen me running or doing my weekly grocery shop. It doesn't stop me from living my life. I am just well aware and always play it careful. I try my best to analyse the movements of strangers when I am out! It doesn't help that my routine is the easiest to follow—you could say that it is a stalker's paradise. I don't think I should have to change for them; I have just become more alert!

I believe some women are jealous of me. Yes, I know that is a big call, but I do believe we are all so judgemental of each other, especially women! We all seem to judge people and make assumptions on how they look, assuming we know—or think we know—what their lives are like. They look at me and see the slim, fit, curvy body my mother blessed me with; long wavy blonde hair; light blue, almost grey, almond-shaped eyes; light golden skin with perfectly contoured make-up and think my life must be easy. At thirty-one years old, I have realised that women want to be me, and men want to fuck me! It's truly that simple. They don't see the life behind the pink lipstick, that there is so much more to me than just my body and looks. They don't think for one second that for some people, make-up is a mask that you wear to hide behind! They don't see the sadness, the fears, the pain, and all the same insecurities I have that they do. They just see me as a plastic skinny blonde. I bet they say to themselves, *Bitch gets everything she wants. I bet she has a man who looks after her and she doesn't have to lift a finger.* They don't realise that because of how I look, I have a constant target on my head!

One day I went to work and was complaining to a woman I had worked with for many years—not even complaining, really; I was just more or less explaining to her how people judged me, and how I felt many women didn't like me. Her response shocked me. It was one of those comments that stick in your mind for life, and I don't believe I will ever forget it!

She told me, "I can tell you right now that I know the reason women automatically don't like you." I asked her why, as I was extremely curious for her reasoning, and she went on to tell me, her voice changing from normal to crude, "Because you are the kind of woman who steals our husbands! That's why!" To this day, I can still see her facial expression when she said almost angrily that I was the one complaining. How rude of me!

Even people close to you can think this of you. My father used to tell me when I was a child that I was a stupid blonde and would have to marry well to get anywhere in life. Comments like that used to upset me and hurt me, but then I realised that most people in my everyday life—teachers, employers, work colleagues, family, and even friends—thought this of me! This became the greatest weapon I had. At least if everyone underestimated you, you could never disappoint.

I grew up in a small town, and now I live in an even smaller town with my husband. I have always liked quiet small towns. I don't like a lot of people or neighbours, and I don't have a lot of friends. Again, I am extremely independent and have a busy, tight schedule. I just don't have time. I have two close old friends, and that's all I need. They are my chosen family.

I don't ever feel lonely when I am alone. I enjoy my time alone—sometimes I think I like it too much! I see the girls in their tribe-packs when I am out and see how much fun they are all having, and then I remind myself how sad it is for them, all the back-stabbing that goes on and how they rely on each other for their happiness instead of themselves.

Our home is a cute 1980s weatherboard three-bedroom house. We have five chickens and a veggie patch. I remember the feeling of joy when we first moved in. We both grew up with nothing and felt so proud and happy of our achievement. I remember feeling that this house was going to be our forever home. We had always dreamed we would renovate to make more space for when we were ready to have children. I am glad we have not reached that achievement, as the pressure I have on me, as a thirty-one-year-old married woman, to have a baby is so overwhelming! Sometimes it feels as if women are just put on this earth as a pleasure outlet for men; then their bodies turn into baby-making machines.

I've always had a fear of having children, and as I get older, the feeling gets stronger. Would I be a good mum, am I too selfish, would our family stay together, am I capable of truly loving that child? Sometimes I don't know if I am capable of truly loving anything. One of my fears is that as soon as I have a baby with my husband, he will leave me. It's silly that I feel like this, for I have never been abandoned before, but it happens … You finally give someone what he wants, and then he seems to move on to the next thing he wants.

A man I worked with once told me the key needs of a man, saying that if you do these three things, your man will never leave or cheat: feed him, fuck him, and thank him! People have always said that men have simple needs, but I didn't realise how easy it actually could be until he said that. I found it humorous, but it did make a lot of sense to me as well. I do use this code in my marriage, as it's my own insecurity that he could one day leave. I work so hard every day in keeping up appearances. I must admit I do make it look easy, even though it's not. My house is always clean, I am always dressed to impress, and I never let other people see my pain or my fears—not even my husband. The entire time I have known him, he has never seen me cry, not one tear. There seems to be only one person in this world so far whom I cannot fool, and that would be my best friend, Kristina. She seems to know things about me before I even realise them!

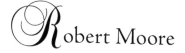obert Moore

WHEN I FIRST met my husband, Robert, my first impression of him was that he was a kind, gentle man who seemed to be everyone's friend. He was always laughing with the boys, loved having a casual beer, and seemed like a laid-back country boy who was easy to get along with. I was immediately attracted to him and those qualities. I'd had all sorts of men in the past, and I didn't want any more bad boys!

I remember the first time my eyes caught his from across the room. I was at a country pub for my friend Kristina's birthday. We were standing out front drinking, and he was wearing a blue flannelette shirt, blue jeans, and black steel-capped boots. He had this nice country boy charm about him, even when he spoke. Robbie is medium height, about a foot taller than I am, with a strong muscular build and scruffy brown hair. With his blue eyes and the week's growth of facial hair he maintains, he is gorgeous to look at!

When we first met, he introduced himself to me when I was standing at the bar waiting for my drink. As he was a smoker, we ended up on the deck outside in the sunshine, chatting about life all afternoon, the conversation just flowing between us. He told me he wanted to get married—he wanted that one person to come home to every night—and then, later on down the track, possibly have children, but he was more interested in the partnership first. I knew that most men say that to lure women, but I wasn't that kind of woman, and I did believe he was telling the truth; he seemed genuine about what he wanted in life. He was not a sleazy man. I had dealt with my fair share of those men, and he certainly was not that type of man!

We started to date, and I noticed how hard he worked at his job. He worked a lot of overtime, trying to get ahead in life. He would tell me, "Work hard now and relax later." He lived by that code. His family consisted of nice, normal people, but earlier on, they had nothing and were extremely poor. He grew up on a dairy farm, and it was an extremely tough life for them! It didn't take me long to realise that Robbie's biggest fear was having nothing. He would tell me he was doing it for our future, for us, but I always knew he was doing it for himself. I was told six months into our relationship from one of his friends that when we first met, Robbie didn't actually think much of me. He thought I was an emotionless Barbie, and his mates had told him to just have fun with me, use me as an outlet! That comment always played in my mind. Men can be disgusting at times! In saying that, he had always treated me with respect, so I never knew if his friend was being genuine or jealous.

We'd dated for just over a year when he proposed to me. The first year of dating, he was very outgoing and enjoyed seeing his friends and going out. That was good, as it gave me a chance to catch up with my girlfriends. We were always actually doing things, but after a couple of years together, he gradually became more of a homebody each day. He couldn't see it, but he was slowly isolating himself—and me—in the process. I started to resent him for this, as I don't do well feeling trapped and confined. He started to become controlling. At the start, I found it sexy; the dominating side was coming out of him, with his getting all jealous and protective over me. It hadn't occurred to me that he had always been this way. He had always done it to me in a way that I never noticed, not even realising he was doing it. I started to learn that he was by far more cunning than any other man I had been with. His personality had always been on the reserved side, unless you knew him, but I started to realise that the reason he was controlling was that he was secretly insecure about me.

Our life became all about going to work and coming home, and that was it. He was happy living like this, but for me it was like Groundhog Day every day. Then I realised that he didn't trust me. I had never done anything to make him think otherwise, but it didn't matter; I couldn't change how he felt. For Robbie, I was a double-edged sword. He had always liked the way I dressed and loved how I looked after myself. To him, I am his trophy, a toy that only he gets to play with. He had always been proud to have me on his arm when we would go out, but he hated how other men would look at and admire me. I could see in his eyes that it drove him crazy. Those are the only times he ever truly compliments me—when we are out and he starts noticing the other men around looking at me. He will be okay for a while, and then he will suddenly decide it's time to go home. Then that's it—the night's over!

We all have sides to us that we don't allow other people to see. I am quite aware of what I am capable of, and I think that's what scares me the most. Sometimes it's the unknown of what people are capable of. In my marriage, like everyone else's, we have our difficulties, but I have never seen my husband snap. How could he be so calm all the time? He might get insecure and paranoid and rush out of a party, but he never actually gets angry. Sometimes I think that if he could read my mind for only one day, he would probably smother me to death in my sleep. I don't have a wandering eye—I honestly love him and see myself spending my life with him—but I have a restless mind and energy that wants so badly to be freed. Feeling trapped and confined doesn't help my situation or my restless mind.

My sex drive has always been higher than Robbie's, and there is nothing wrong with that. I have always thought I have a woman's body with a man's brain. The three keys to a man's needs are essentially what I think would keep me happy—or at least satisfied! It's funny how females are given hints about how to keep a man happy, but what about us women? Who makes our lunch? Who thanks us? Men are so tired when they get home from work to even think about anything other than when dinner is ready! They eat and then continue to veg on the couch while you clean up from dinner. Quite amazing, really. Then once you finish that job, they climb on you and thrust until they are finished. Then the next job you have is to get out of bed and clean up from the mess they have just made. I think it is quite humorous when you really think about it. Maybe I am too cutthroat or even cynical. Things either are or they aren't—there truly is no in between. Once again, I am not complaining. This is just how I see things!

I felt my husband was my safe choice. We all choose the people in our lives for whatever reason. I believe we do choose our parents from the time we are conceived. We choose these people to teach us lessons, obvious ones we didn't learn in our past lives. I believe that our personalities are partially picked before we have even arrived in this world, that our genetics and how we are raised form the shape of the person we become. I am not saying that if your father is a rapist, you will become a rapist. What I am saying is that we all have traits of our parents and exhibit their mannerisms.

I know it would take something big for Robbie to leave me. He is a lazy and content man when it comes to those things. With every choice in life, there is a compromise. I chose security over excitement. I didn't have any regrets, as I knew that one day my husband would make a terrific father to my children.

We got married five years ago in December, barefoot on the beach and surrounded by candles. It was a private romantic ceremony. I had always dreamed of getting married barefoot; I felt it was the last freedom I had before I was completely tied down. I wore a light flowing white spaghetti strap gown and had a flower crown sitting on my curled free-flowing hair. I remember how happy I felt when the celebrant said, "You may kiss the bride!" It was such a rush of joy. As everyone tossed red and white rose petals over us, it was magical.

Part of my problem is that I have a hormone imbalance and possibly borderline personality disorder as well. I have never been tested, but I am always trying to keep track of it, so I keep a diary and analyse my feelings for the day, referring back to the previous month in order to analyse and reason with myself as to why I feel like this. The reason for this is because for four days a month, I find life almost physically impossible. My sexual desires become so strong, and my thoughts become so out of control. I find myself sneaking off to the bathroom at ridiculous hours in the night to relieve myself just so I can go to sleep. It doesn't sound that bad, but if I don't, then throbbing begins. I don't have a sex-addiction or anything. It's just my hormones playing up! I sometimes beg for it to go away, as it literally drives me crazy. It doesn't help that my husband doesn't believe in having sex anywhere other than the bed. Okay, okay, I know it's not that bad, and yes, I *have* been married for five years. I have never said a word, and I do hear some of my co-workers in our lunchroom complaining that they don't have sex at all, so I cannot complain! It's just that for once I would love for him to go down on me, or just put me up against a wall, or, even crazier, have sex on our new couch! I seriously have had the same sex in the same place for the past five years—same bed, same room.

I probably sound depressing, but I am not trying to be. I just thought having the simple domestic goddess housewife lifestyle would keep me busy enough not to think about it—and that I would be happy. I think many people would be happy being in my marriage. I'm just not convinced that I can be this person forever. I told myself so many times that he was right for me and that I needed this life, but I find myself so lonely and bored in his company.

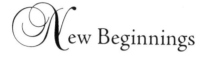ew Beginnings

ONE YEAR AGO ...

My entire life started to change about a year ago. It all began with my work. I started receiving job promotions and pay rises unexpectedly, and I hadn't even asked for or applied for them. I didn't really want more responsibility. As I said earlier, I didn't give a shit about the company—or my job, for that matter! People were losing their jobs around me, and for some crazy reason, I was getting promoted and paid more. I couldn't work it out. I just kept thinking to myself not to get too comfortable, as my number would be up shortly. I felt bad for the people I worked with. They were great people, and they all had huge mortgages and children to feed, whereas I didn't ... Yet I still had my job. I was in a good monetary position with Robbie. We got a bargain with our home and had minimal owing on our mortgage, no children, two good incomes, and not a lot of outgoings.

On 26 May, I received an email from the director of the company. In that email he had asked and then booked into my daily scheduler advising that I had a meeting with him at three o'clock that day. I wasn't too upset, as I was well aware that my days were limited. On my lunch break that day, I decided to spend my time outside. It was a beautiful and fresh sunny autumn day, and I decided to call Robbie and let him know that my day had finally come. He felt the same I as did and told me not to worry. I had a great resume and connections, and I would get another job soon.

Three o'clock rolled around reasonably quickly, and I started to make my way to the meeting. I took the lift up to the top, the twenty-third floor of the building. I had never even seen the director of the company before, and I had worked there for the past six years. Seems strange, but I never had any reasons to, and his face certainly wasn't splashed around the lunchroom, so I had no idea what to expect.

The doors to the lift opened, and as I entered the room, I could see an overly large sophisticated brushed oak desk, with a large room with tinted windows directly behind it. The nameplate on the hardwood stained door read Director Kevin Jacobs, which was the name I had read on the email I received earlier, so I knew I was in the right place.

I walked up to the reception desk and greeted the receptionist, who was wearing a name tag that read Heather. She was a beautiful brunette woman around my age, maybe slightly younger, and she was wearing a headset. She held her fake smile as I told her that I had a meeting at three with Kevin Jacobs. She told me to take a seat and said he wouldn't be long.

I wasn't waiting long at all when Heather stood up and told me, "Kevin is ready to see you now." When she half opened the door for me, I started to enter the room, and she quickly closed the door behind me.

I continued into the luxurious but masculine-looking office. It had expensive four-metre-high black velvet drapes that were drawn and a large solid hardwood desk sitting in the centre, with a computer sitting on it. I noticed that there was a couch off to the side with cushions on it, a matching twelve-seat solid wood dining table with tall black leather chairs, and a door that led into another room behind the table. He had big black matte plant pots with beautiful large bangalow palms and my personal favourite, fiddle-leaf figs, planted in the corners of the room. His office looked like something you would see in a magazine.

Kevin Jacobs was a powerful and wealthy man, and not at all as I imagined him to be. He was tall with a masculine build, he had broad shoulders and solid legs and arms. I could see how toned he was, even though he was wearing a dark navy blue suit. He had lightly tanned skin, light brown hair, gorgeous dark brown eyes, and I would say he was in his early forties. He had a strong stance and held himself in a confident manner; his sexy ruggedness was most attractive. He was certainly more than attractive for an older man. I would say *hot!* An extremely sexy man!

He walked over to me and shook my hand. After he introduced himself to me, he then sat me down on the sofa and asked me why I believed he had asked to see me. He was so incredibly good-looking that I felt like a giggly little schoolgirl. It was awful! I laughed nervously and said, "I think you are letting me know that my time is up."

He laughed and said, "No, quite the opposite. I've invited you here to give you an opportunity." I laughed nervously once again. "I understand that you are a qualified accountant and that what I am about to say isn't really in your line of work, but I would like to invite you to become my full-time assistant. Before you give me an answer, let me explain. I have had many PAs in the past—and don't get me wrong; they are great at scheduling my appointments and my day—but I need someone who knows my day and also understands all the lingo, someone who can guide me through the meetings I have and be able to give me financial advice on what decisions I should make on behalf of the Firm. Day in and day out, I work and meet with many different people who hold a lot of power, and I have critical meetings where every suit in the room has his own hidden agenda. People always have their hands in my pockets, and I don't trust the pack of them! What do you think, Ella? Would you be my eyes and ears?"

I didn't know what to say. I'd told myself I was going to the twenty-third floor to get fired, and here I was getting a completely different job role. I was in shock and just sat there in silence.

"I have looked over your file," he continued. "Currently you are on $80K plus super a year. If you take this position, I will start you off on a $130K package plus super. Look it's a lot more hours, but I do believe that this is a very generous offer. I have been watching you, Ella, and I really want you on my team! What's it going to take?"

I couldn't help but laugh in my head as I thought about his comment that he had been "watching me"! That was a concern. I could visualise myself spinning around in my chair and daydreaming out my window. I agreed I would take on the job—I couldn't think of even one reason to decline his offer. Something about him made me feel that I couldn't really say no to him anyway. I was constantly dreaming about doing something spontaneous, less routine, and I felt that the universe had finally listened to what I had been craving and trying to suppress … I was going to accept this opportunity that had been placed in front of me.

Kevin smiled and seemed enthusiastic about my answer. He then went on to tell me more details about my job description. My current 8:00 a.m. to 5:30 p.m. work hours would now be 7:00 a.m. until 6:00 p.m. The company would provide breakfast, lunch, and snacks. He told me that breakfast would be delivered no later than 7:10 a.m. I would have my choice of food, and then we'd spend the first hour together, organising and planning all his meetings for the day. Then we'd sort through all the messages that had been left for him overnight and prioritise the urgency and the nature of the meetings. We would revise the day again after we had lunch, as in those hours, many dramas may have arisen that needed to take priority. We'd always stop and have morning and afternoon tea, whether we were in the office or not. If we were out, we might stop for something at a café and then eat it in a park at the full expense of the company.

He then asked me if I would be able to start my new position tomorrow morning. I agreed, and he explained to me where I needed to park my car. He told me that before I left his office that day, he needed me to select on his computer what I would like to eat for breakfast the following day. I was so excited and felt like a child at Christmas. I love food, especially when I don't have to make it!

I browsed through the selection on his computer. I got my typical breakfast: antioxidant-rich high-protein oat and fruit smoothie. He told me as he laughed that he thought it was quite amusing watching how excited I was about selecting food for breakfast. He thanked me and then held his hand out to shake mine, asking, "Do you think you could handle hanging out with me for eleven hours every day?"

I cheekily replied, "I'm sure it will be fine. You don't look like a serial killer or anything."

He laughed and replied, "What does a serial killer look like?"

I don't know why, but I said, "A monster!"

He burst into laughter and said, "True," clamping his hands together and continuing to laugh.

I couldn't help but slap, punch, and kick myself on the inside! What a stupid and weird thing to say... What was wrong with me? I think nerves just took over me.

I shook his hand, and he wished me a good day. After leaving his office, I made my way back down to the lifts. I got off for the last time at the seventeenth floor and went back to my now-old desk. I packed up all my belongings.

When I got home later, Robbie gave me his usual greeting kiss and we sat out the back patio. I was drinking my green tea, whilst Robbie had his usual coffee and smoke. When I sat down, Robbie asked me about my day. I started to explain the meeting with Kevin the director, and I told him that I had been promoted to a different job role and what the job actually entailed. I then told him about my new more than generous salary package. His first response was shock, and as he took the last drag of his cigarette, he said, "You're like a cat with nine lives with this job. I don't know how you do it, Ella. Had you even seen or met this Kevin guy before?"

I told him I had never seen Kevin before then, which was a lie, for I had realized I'd seen him a few times in the lobby. Each time I did, he was surrounded by attractive young women. Robbie told me he thought it was weird. He told me that I should try it for a couple days and see how it went; otherwise, if I didn't like it, he told me to just quit and get another job elsewhere.

I couldn't help but lie awake that night, nervous and excited about the next day. I had a positive feeling about it, but I just couldn't get the thoughts out of my head. *Why me? Why was I chosen for this role? What did he see in me? What had people told him about me? Was there an ulterior motive behind it?*

I tried to relax my thinking. It took a while, but I eventually fell asleep.

CHAPTER 4

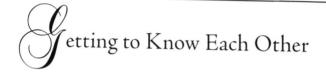

etting to Know Each Other

MY MORNING STARTED as usual. I got Robbie ready for work, and then I had limited time to get myself ready to leave, as I had to be there an hour earlier than usual. Luckily, I didn't have to pack my lunch or make my breakfast anymore, which was most refreshing. It was also a strange feeling that someone else was actually helping me get ready for once!

I started to get dressed for work, rolling my black stockings up to my thighs, putting on my tight-fitting black office dress, and sliding my feet into my three-inch black leather Mary Jane heels. I got my coat and drove to the office, using the directions Kevin had given me the previous day regarding how to access my new parking spot. I made my way to the top car park and could see Kevin's car spot, as it had his name and position on a lavish metal plaque on the wall. I found a blank spot and decided it would be safe to park my car, as I wasn't sure who else would park up there.

Probably within a minute of parking, a stylish sleek white four-seater Maserati drove into the car park. It reversed and parked into the car space, I drive a Toyota and am not usually that interested in cars, but even I can say that this car got my attention.

A moment later, Kevin got out of the car, retrieved his black leather briefcase and coat from the back seat, and walked over to my car. He opened the door and leaned his body against it. "Are you ready for day one, Ella?" I nodded and followed him through the car park to the entrance door of the building.

We both said our good mornings to Heather and continued to walk through to his office. As I entered it, I noticed that it looked different than it did yesterday, when I had had the meeting with him. Kevin picked up a remote, and with a click of a button, the heater turned on, the four-metre-high drapes that were drawn started to open, and I could see that he had a magnificent view of the ocean. I saw that now there was a desk with a computer on both sides of the room, facing each other, whereas the previous day there was only one desk in the centre of the room. He showed me the bathroom behind the door I had noticed yesterday. My desk was the one on the right-hand side of the room. The room had a clean and sophisticated feel about it. I liked it.

There was a knock on the door. Kevin called out to the person to come in, and a young man from the local cafe walked into the room to drop off our breakfast. We sat down at my new desk with our breakfast, and Kevin started to introduce me to my new job role, showing me how to use the computer system with my newly linked iPad, iPhone, and all my new passwords. My new position required me to wear a headset, which I had never previously worn. It was tiny and not noticeable; it just clipped onto my ear. As we unpacked our meal, I couldn't help but be impressed with his breakfast. I care so much about my heath, and it's good to see other people doing the same. He had ordered a protein shake and sliced ham and smashed avocado on two slices of sourdough. We ate as Kevin explained to me the different appointments and meetings he had scheduled for the day, thoroughly covering the importance of certain people and the roles they played.

Eight in the morning came around quickly, and we had the first appointment for the day. The schedule was somewhat mismatched, but the day was broken up because he had meetings in the office as well as out-of-office meetings. He explained to me that he went mad confined in an office all day and liked to stretch his legs, so he told me to keep that in mind when booking his appointments. We had the first two appointments in office, which lasted until around ten thirty, and then Kevin told me to get my handbag, iPhone, and iPad and follow him. He grabbed his keys, and we walked through the office to the car park exit door.

When we reached Kevin's car, he unlocked it and told me to jump in. I opened the passenger door and put my handbag on the floor, sliding my body across the leather into a seated position. I began to take it all in. His car still had that new leather car smell, but it also had a sexy smell like masculine cologne. It looked like a race car on the inside, with tight leather seats and lots of gadgets and lights. Kevin put his briefcase and coat in the back seat. As he got in the car, I could smell his skin. It was so sexy. I could smell it in the car before, but when he got in it, the smell became so much stronger. As he was driving, he started to ask me questions about my life. He told me he'd noticed my wedding rings and asked me how long I had been married. I told him five years. I noticed his wedding ring, but I didn't ask. It was just small talk back and forth, but it flowed easily.

We had a good forty minutes until our next appointment, and Kevin drove up to a hip and healthy cafe in a strip of shops right in front of the ocean. It was called The Fat Bird Can't Fly. Kevin parked directly in front and then asked me, "Are you ready for morning tea? I did notice we eat similarly, and I think you'll like this place. They always do a good and healthy tucker."

I was only four hours into my new job and loving life! I thought, *This guy is so cool. I cannot believe I'm getting paid to do this. I'd probably do this for free, to be honest.*

We both ordered a freshly squeezed juice. I ordered a banana chia gluten-free muffin, and he ordered a sourdough toasted ham, cheese, and tomato sandwich. I let him know that I have a sensitivity to gluten so I avoid it at all costs, adding that I don't eat meat or dairy either. When I told him, he didn't seem too surprised, which was a surprise for me, and it was actually nice, as people in the past were always making fun of my dietary requirements. We sat outside on the benches and ate our morning tea and chatted as I watched the waves roll onto the beach in the distance.

The next meeting we had was only around a twenty-minute drive away, which went quickly considering I was hanging out with a stranger. The first meet-and-greets we had were more one-on-one, and he had me sit in on every meeting and take notes for him. Afterwards, I would be arranging future meetings for him. He also expressed to me that there was a meeting with about forty members once a month. It was a big deal, with no assistants or females allowed to attend, but he told me he would like to change that arrangement!

Before I knew it, the workday was over. It was 5:50 p.m., and Kevin sat me down and asked me if I had enjoyed my first day with him, also asking me if I had any questions or concerns regarding my new position. We lightly chatted until it was time for me to make my way home.

On my way home, I couldn't stop thinking about my day. I knew that when I got home, it would be a mad rush, as even though my hours had increased at work, I still had dinners and lunches to prepare. Unfortunately for me, I knew it wouldn't even cross Robbie's mind to think of helping me. I thought long and hard on that fifty-minute drive home, wanting to tell Robbie as least as possible about my new job. Yes, it sounds bad, but I knew it would cause trouble and start a fight. Robbie would get jealous of Kevin and insecure about himself, and I really couldn't be bothered, to be honest! I had enjoyed my day and my new job, and I had made my decision and was sticking to it.

I got home, greeted Robbie with a kiss, put my things down, and asked him how his day was. We did not do our usual sit-down, as it was almost seven and dinner wasn't even prepped. He asked me about my day, and I told him I would tell him all about it during dinner. I did a cheat dinner, throwing a frozen pie and a packet of quinoa in the microwave and turning on the oven. I thawed the pie for a few minutes and then popped it into the oven, steaming some veggies to serve with it.

As we sat down to dinner, Robbie was straight away asking me many questions about my day. Kevin intrigued him; I could tell by the amount of questions that he was asking me about him. He even wanted a description of what he looked like! I told him bits and pieces but played down everything about this man, as I did not want Robbie to get protective or even envious of him. He asked me what type of car he drove, and I told him a sporty white one. As I have never taken any interest in cars, I could get away with saying a comment like that. Even though I had a lack of knowledge about cars, even I knew that a Maserati was a sought-after vehicle to men.

I cleaned up from dinner and prepared Robbie's lunch for the following day. I was so relieved that it was Thursday night and I only had one more day left of working. I made my nightly chamomile tea before going to bed. It could have been my paranoia, but I did think Robbie wasn't convinced about my new job. I could tell by the way he had been acting. I climbed into bed, sinking my head into the pillow and instantly starting to drift off. I felt Robbie start thrusting behind me in a spooning position. He may not have a high sex drive, but when he was in the mood, there was no stopping him, so I just went with it!

He took my arm and tried to drag my body on top of his. I told him that I didn't feel like being on top tonight, so he let go of my arm and climbed on top of me. I personally don't like being on top during sex. It does absolutely nothing for me—we are all so different and have different needs, but I have always liked my partners to be on top. I feel like I am alone up there and may as well have sex with myself, by myself! A strong sexually dominating lover turns me on. It doesn't matter which position we are in, as long as he is in full control. It increases my chances of reaching an orgasm. My friends have asked me if I ever fake orgasms, and I always tell them no. Why would I pretend that I am enjoying something that I am not? I don't want him to think, *Oh, wow, she really enjoyed that. I'll do that next time.* No way. I am not going through that again! Sex has always felt very different to me compared to how I hear other people portray it to be. It's not just with my husband; it has been this way with all my past lovers. It is almost like a need, then a want! I put my head back and stare at the ceiling, and every thought leaves my body instantly. It's an amazing feeling. It's the only time my brain ever shuts down. I can see only darkness, and I am finally numb.

The next week of work seemed to fly by, with lots of meet-and-greets. I had only two weeks until that big meeting Kevin wanted to sneak me into. That had been playing on my mind a lot as well, how I was going to sneak into a room of forty-plus men without being noticed. It was funny because I can't walk anywhere without someone noticing me. I knew that I would think of something. I just hoped it wouldn't be on the spot, as those plans never go down that well.

One day, only a week into my new job, stood out amongst most of my days, as this particular day was when I met Kevin's wife. The day had gotten off to a normal start. We had had breakfast, running through the appointments for the day. The next appointment was in an hour's time, and we were both catching up on paperwork. Heather, the receptionist, called me to let me know that Kim Jacobs, aka Kevin's wife, was at reception, wanting to see Kevin. Heather explained, "I just wanted to check that you aren't on a conference call before I send her in."

I let Kevin know, and he told me to send her in as he rolled his eyes, stressfully rubbing his eyebrow into his forehead, and said, "Here we go!"

I was so intrigued. I guess when you meet people and they are partnered up, you cannot help but wonder about their partners, who they are and what they look like. We create these images in our minds of these people. Kevin didn't have any photos of his wife in the office and had never previously mentioned her. The only reason I knew he was married was the ring on his wedding finger, other than that, I wouldn't have realised. I had wondered what kind of woman he would be married to. I imagined his wife to be in her late thirties, slim, brunette with tanned skin, and stunning to look at.

She walked into the room in a huff, with her nose stuck up to the ceiling, wearing Prada shoes and carrying a Versace handbag on her arm. Kim was not at all what I expected. I mean, Kevin is extremely good-looking and a kind man. Kim looked rather old. She had thin black hair that they had tried to make look thicker when they blow-waved it. She looked as if either she had had an extremely stressful life or dabbled with drugs. She was skeleton thin and had no body shape whatsoever—her clothes just hung off her. She had a certain harshness to her. I could feel her energy straight away, nothing but cold.

She trotted straight into the centre of the room, standing in between both our desks, and then looked at Kevin and slowly and sarcastically waved and said hi to him. She then looked over at me and started to laugh. With an irate tone in her voice, she said, "It's finally happened, Kevin! Only took you fifteen years of running this company to do it—you finally hired a whore."

Kevin exploded out of his seat, took her tightly by the arm, and said to her, "What the fuck is wrong with you, Kim? Shut your fucking mouth! What do you want? I am working and can't be fucked with your shit today."

Kim laughed once again, tried to wriggle his hand off her arm, and said to him, "I want money. Write me a cheque. I want to go shopping!"

Kevin slowly let go of her arm, sat down at his desk, opened his top left drawer, and pulled out his chequebook. Once he had finished writing the cheque, he ripped the paper out of the book and remained seated in his chair. He held the cheque in his hand in the air and waited for her to lean over his desk to try to grab it out of his hand. As she went to do so, he continued to hold it tightly. Kim tried but could not get enough grip to take it. He dragged her by the arm towards his chest and whispered in her ear, "You've almost spent your yearly allowance, Kim. Once it's gone, it's gone."

Kim snatched the cheque and rushed straight towards the exit door. She stopped, looked back in my direction, and said, "You know, he only hired you so he could fuck you! Once he gets what he wants, you'll be gone like the rest of them." She looked over at Kevin in a panic and hurriedly opened the door, squeezing her body through it in a hurry, as she clearly couldn't get out of the room fast enough, and slammed the door behind her.

I just sat there, not really surprised by her reaction to me. I mean, I was used to women hating me, but I *was* surprised by Kevin's reaction to his wife. He defended me when she made that comment about me; no one had ever stood up for me in my life as he did! Then I was surprised that there was no love there for one another—nothing. The hatred they clearly felt for each other was senseless. It made me wonder what could happen between a husband and wife to make them hate each other to that level!

As soon as she escaped the room, Kevin walked over to me and leaned his bum against my desk, facing me. He started to apologise to me for his wife's behaviour and how she had spoken to me. I shrugged it off and told him not to worry about it. I could tell he felt awful about it. He explained to me that he was not a violent man—and he hated my seeing him like that—but his wife drove him insane. He went on to tell me that he was forced to marry her when he was twenty-eight years old and he had always hated her. The business had been in his family's name for over four generations, and he wanted to take over from his father, but his father told him there was one condition: he had to marry a woman of the same stature as him. Kim came from old money as well. Kevin's and Kim's fathers had done business together for over twenty years and were good friends, so it only made sense to his father and he told me that he felt his marriage was a business deal.

He went on to tell me, "My mother tried so hard to talk my father out of it. She could see how unhappy I was going to be, and how cold Kim was, but there is no reasoning with my father! So fifteen years later, here we are."

I felt so awful for him. He wanted to take over the family business and prove himself to his father so badly that he married someone he didn't like. That was his sacrifice. I could see the same loneliness in his eyes that I have often felt. We often sacrifice something to get what we want. It's not until later that we realise what we end up sacrificing is the thing we actually needed in the first place.

We finished what we were doing and started to head off for the meeting we had. As we got into his car, I couldn't help but think how natural and comfortable I felt with him. I was so drawn to him. I had spent the past few weeks with him, and I hadn't seen it until now, but I could now see clearly that we shared the same sadness.

We went to the next meeting and then stopped at The Fat Bird Can't Fly for our morning tea. This was quickly becoming my favourite stop. Their food was delicious, and the seats with the view were too hard to resist. I have always had a thing for the ocean. It intrigues me ... I find myself staring at the waves, watching the giant ones crash down with force and then turn to such a still calmness. I have always found it so exhilarating and serene at the same time.

We sat at the outside tables on the lawn to eat, and it was so peaceful and calm. I knew there had to be a reason this man had come into my life! For the first time in a long time, I felt my life had some sort of purpose and I wasn't alone anymore.

Within weeks, we were having a sexy lingo back and worth. We had this flirty energy towards one another. It felt so natural and comfortable, and he didn't at all feel like my boss! It was strange because he felt like my friend, the kind of friend you would joke around with, play fight, poke and punch, a friend I could say anything to, with no judgement whatsoever. He asked me one day as we were driving in his car back to the office what type of music I listen to. At first, I laughed and thought it was a bit strange. "What does that have to do with anything?" I asked. He then went on to tell me that he believes music comes from the soul and you can tell a person by the music they listen to.

I probably looked like a pop diva kind of girl, but that was far from the truth. I only like male singers. I don't know why I have always felt this way. It's almost as if I don't trust or believe women when they sing! I took my phone out of my handbag, connected my phone to the Bluetooth of his car, and opened my Spotify account. He laughed and said, "This will be interesting." I started to play my music, and he kept laughing at me. I told him that if he didn't stop laughing, I would turn it off. He took one hand off the steering wheel and grabbed the back of my hair, running his fingers through my hair as he was driving, and said, "I'm not laughing because I think your music is stupid. I'm laughing because it's not what I expected. This is why I love hanging out with you each and every day! You look like one girl, but underneath that skin, you are someone completely different." He let go of my hair and put both hands back on the steering wheel, starting to bob his head and tap his fingers on the steering wheel along with the music, wearing a cheeky smile. "You intrigue me, Ella Jade."

I listen to two very different types of music, depending on my mood. Sexy country, as I like to call it, is not country music with thick Southern accents. It has an upbeat modern flow to it. I like to sing along in my car sometimes, and it makes me feel sexy and confident. If I'm feeling anything else, I like to listen to nineties rock. I turn it up loud and just scream it out. It's my favourite, and it can truly change my mood and bring me back to a semi state of happiness.

As we got out of the car back at the office, he half leaned over the car, twisting his back and holding his door, and said, "You are so hot to look at, Ella. You have this incredible body, and then you have this random man's brain!" We both laughed, and he closed his car door, shaking his head in disbelief. I couldn't help but agree with his comment—I most definitely do have a man's brain.

As we walked through the car park back to the office, he started pushing, poking, and joking around with me. It was so cute, the friendship that was developing between the two of us. I could feel that Kevin was quickly becoming my weakness. I found it funny that in the short time I had been hanging out with Kevin, he had already picked up on these funny little quirks in my personality, whereas I had been with Robbie for seven years, married for five years, and he had never noticed these things about me.

CHAPTER 5

*T*he Big Meeting

THE DAY OF the big meeting had finally come, and I was nervous as all hell. We headed over to the building where this meeting was held every month. Kevin tried to reassure me that everything would be fine and that they would let me stay in the meeting, saying that he would sort everything out. He said he wouldn't make a fool out of both of us, but I was sure he was trying to reassure himself, not me. I didn't know what to expect; the only thing I could imagine was a room full of rich old men arguing for two hours straight.

We took the lift up to the twenty-first floor. As we stepped out of the lift, there was an ear-piecing amount of noise carrying through the foyer. It was coming from all the young female and male assistants sitting along the walls of the foyer with their iPads and phones, talking over each other and trying to schedule and reschedule appointments for their employers for the day. Kevin had told me that it was old school and only the men were allowed into this meeting, with no assistants or non-members allowed. Kevin wasn't even allowed to take a piece of paper and pen into the meeting. It was very strict, and they were all paranoid. They obviously had a lot to hide.

I walked in the conference room behind Kevin, almost as if his body were my shield. We managed to make our way halfway around the table before one man noticed me. Then all the men in the room bounded out of their chairs and started yelling different things at Kevin: "Get her out!," "She's not allowed in here, Kevin!," "We don't care who you are—it's just not allowed!," and "Who do you think you are?"

Kevin started laughing at them, telling them to calm and sit down, trying to diffuse the situation. He asked them, "What's the real problem here? Why can't I have her here?"

One man in his mid to late fifties stood up and said, "Because she could repeat or record our conversations and use the information later to blackmail us—or release the information to other sources. I just don't trust her!"

Kevin tried desperately to reassure them that I was not going to be recording their conversations and I was most definitely not wearing a wire. It was so ridiculous. They were all so paranoid and acting like five-year-old children, but what Kevin was doing was not working. I needed to help him; I couldn't cope with watching these men attack him. I was starting to panic. So … I did it!

I stood strong and waved my hands, yelling out to everyone to be quiet. I told them that they were being ridiculous. I wasn't wearing a wire and said that I would prove it. I started undressing immediately. My heart was racing, but I didn't care! First I took off my jacket and threw it on the floor, unzipped my dress from the side and let it slowly fall off my body to the floor, and then stepped my black three-inch leather side buckle Mary Jane heels out of the dress. I was left standing there in my thigh-high black stockings with my matching burgundy lace push-up bra and boy-leg panties. I did a slow twirl, walking in a circle, and said, "See, not wearing any wires."

I swear you could have heard a pin drop—it was that silent. Clearly, not one man in the whole room knew what to say. I could feel their beady eyes on me! I looked over at Kevin next to me, and he was just as shocked and kept staring at me with his mouth wide open, speechless. I then looked around the room and asked, "Are we going to have a problem, gentlemen, or can I please get dressed now and take a seat?" They all started nodding at me with their stunned faces and saying yes repeatedly. Some even clapped awkwardly. It was one of the biggest adrenaline rushes I had ever experienced in my life! I felt my heart pounding in my chest, and I felt a sudden rush of confidence and power within.

I got my dress off the floor and quickly put it back on as I started to walk over to Kevin's chair and put my jacket back on. Kevin stood behind me and got the meeting under way. I tried to ascertain as much information as I possibly could, but the adrenaline was rushing through me. It was so strong that I found it hard to concentrate. The meeting went on for around an hour and a half, and it was all political matters dealing with the reserve bank and interest rates. To be honest, it was actually boring.

The meeting ended, and everyone started to head to the door. As I got to the door, all the PAs were looking at me. I could tell by their facial expressions that they were wondering how the hell I managed to get in there and stay in there.

Kevin was silent the entire way back to the car. I was trying to work out what thoughts were going through his head, but I couldn't. I was extremely nervous. I knew I had crossed the line by stripping off almost naked, but I didn't know what else to do, and now I was feeling terrified of how he had taken it. We got into his car, and Kevin started to drive back to the office.

We were only five minutes from our building, and not one word had been spoken yet. All of a sudden, Kevin dramatically pulled the car over into a small dodgy alleyway, screeching the tyres in the process. He stopped the car, put the gear shifter into park, and flicked the handbrake on. He twisted his body to face mine and put his left hand behind his ear, holding his head. He put his right hand on my chin, holding it lightly, and said to me with a mischievous look on his face, "You are fucking crazy, Ella Jade! I can't believe you did that. Do you even know who some of those guys are? You are crazy. I love it!" He started to chuckle to himself, and then he sat back straight in his chair with his head resting firmly into the headrest, looking towards the ceiling. "That was the craziest thing I have seen in all my years in this business!"

I felt an overwhelming feeling, as if something had finally sparked inside me—as if I was finally alive! I felt sexy, dangerous, and powerful, all at the same time, and I felt as if no one could stop me or get in my way. We went back to the office, and all afternoon I could feel Kevin's eyes watching me. I would look out of the corner of my eye and see him just sitting at his desk, staring directly over at me. He was looking at me in a way that he had never looked at me before. As he watched me all afternoon, I wished that I could figure what he was thinking. I started to chew the ends of my nails, as I was getting anxious, but not because he was staring at me. I was starting to get frightened of what was happening to me, but at the same time, the constant state of supremacy made me feel so erotic, and I wasn't quite ready to give that up just yet!

Six o'clock took so long to come around. I couldn't wait to get out of the office. With the feelings I felt for Kevin, I needed to get out of there and far, far away from him. I wished Kevin a nice night and apologised as I was leaving for the day. I made my way to my car and then home. I was so incredibly aroused at this moment that I just had to get home. I could feel the domesticated boring wife stature starting to slip.

As soon as I got through the front door of our house, I grabbed Robbie's face with one hand on each side of his face and held it firmly. I started to kiss him passionately. He moved his head back and smiled at me, saying, "Someone's happy to see me." It didn't help that today was day one out of four for my hormones. He started to kiss my neck and said to me, "Bedroom now. Let's go!" We went off to the bedroom and had the best sex I think we had ever had in the whole five years of our marriage. After we finished, I dressed and then went back into the kitchen and made our dinner.

Robbie held his gaze on me the entire evening, and as we sat down to eat, he held his hands together to his face with straight elbows on the table, a curious look upon his face. "So how was your day today, Ella? Anything interesting happen?" He seemed extremely inquisitive.

I replied, "It was good. Not a lot, really. Not anything other than the normal."

"Really! You're telling me that you burst into the house like that, you jump on me, we have incredible sex … and then you're telling me nothing happened today."

"It's just that my hormones are playing up again, Robbie— that's all! Every once in a while, can't I jump on my husband when I come home from work?" He nodded in agreement.

We finished dinner, and I hurried off to the kitchen to tidy up and try to avoid him and his questions. Then I immediately made my way to bed to avoid any further interrogations from him.

I realised that I had now been working for Kevin for around eight months, and every day I looked forward to going to work. I couldn't wait for the weekends to go fast enough so I could be back at work. Monday morning with Kevin … It was as if something changed inside me and I finally had a purpose. Over the past six months, I had been accepted into the monthly meeting without any qualms; all of the men included me in their discussions and even asked me for my opinions. Some of them even started calling the office, wanting to send through private documents for me to look over to check the authenticity of them. The other PAs were so envious of me, but I didn't care. I felt important by his side.

I believe it was at this point that Robbie started truly noticing the change in me. I was feeling confident and growing stronger every day. I started getting our dinners delivered and hired a cleaner once a week for the day to clean the entire house and to do all of our washing. We were both earning amazing money, and I couldn't understand why it was still up to me to be doing everything around the house. I was making more money than he was, and if I wanted to spend it, so be it!

The phone calls started coming home with me—some nights I would be receiving phone calls until eight at night, wanting me to organise last minute meetings, book flights, give advice, and look over their private documents. It didn't matter if it was Friday night or Sunday morning; I was getting contacted. Kevin was unsure about Robbie. I hadn't told him much about him, so he would always message me first, and then I would call him back straight away, unless it was detrimentally urgent, and then he would call me directly.

Every year we spend Christmas Day with Robbie's family. We go to his mother's house, and his whole family congregates, including his siblings, nieces, nephews, and cousins. It's a full-on day. After lunch, it's always present time. We all have to sit down to watch as Robbie's mother, who dressed as Santa's little helper, hand out presents from under the tree. As my phone started to ring at the same time, I looked down at my phone and then immediately looked over at Robbie awkwardly.

Robbie asked me to ignore it so we could watch the kids open their presents. I told him, "I can't ignore it, Robbie. It must be urgent! He only ever rings if it's urgent."

I got up from the couch, walked away from everyone, and answered my phone. It was Kevin. He needed to ask me a few questions about some documents I had been working on. He told me that something important had come up and he needed to know something in particular. I took my iPad out of my handbag and got into the document. I looked over it and guided him through the information he required. I tried to get off the phone as quickly as possible, as I could feel many eyes on me. I wished Kevin a merry Christmas and hung up the phone, heading back to the couch next to Robbie.

As I sat down, Robbie's whole family began shooting me filthy looks. His mother moved over to us and handed me my present, starting to lecture me how inappropriate it was for me to take a work phone call on Christmas Day. His family all started to get involved and joined in ganging up on me, telling me my job was getting out of control and my relationship with my employer was inappropriate for him to think it would be okay to contact me on Christmas Day. His sister told me I should have just ignored the phone call. My mother in-law then snarled that I should reconsider my new job, as it was only a job, and I should start concentrating on a family with her son!

I felt like shouting "Happy Christmas, everyone!" His family had always been overbearing, and it didn't help that there were so many of them. In a debate or argument, they were a force to be reckoned with. Robbie was also the favourite, so it didn't matter what I did—I would never be good enough for their precious Robbie. I just brushed them off and tried not to take it personally, as I have learned in the past that when you try to stand up for yourself, it makes things so much worse. They were always right! In this case, they probably were right. But in saying that, they had no idea how this job made me feel. Robbie did, and that's why he couldn't stand it!

Not long after Christmas, Robbie started pestering me for a baby. He started making comments throughout our dinners and randomly trying to touch me on the couch when we were watching a movie. I felt it was becoming a repetitive conversation he would bring up, which would escalate into a fight. He had never cared in the past, and all of a sudden, he wanted a baby. I felt that it was because he was losing control of me and that a baby would be a way he could regain control over me. I fought him every step of the way. I was finally finding myself, and I wasn't ready or interested in a baby right now.

Chapter 6

The Pink Owl Foundation Ball

KEVIN HAD A foundation he'd set up on his own to raise money and awareness for kids with a rare form of leukaemia. Kevin's sister Jodie had died from it as a child, and he'd watched her die a slow and painful death. He didn't want other families to have to go through the same pain. It was called The Pink Owl Foundation, as Jodie's favourite colour was pink, and as she started to fade away, she started to have an increased connection to owls. The owls helped her through colouring and plush toys, and it seemed to take her mind off what was really going on, so Kevin felt it was an appropriate fit. Once a year, Kevin held a fully catered ball for all the A-listers. Everyone who was anyone or had money was there, and he put every cent raised from the night into the charity.

I was aware that the annual event was tonight, so I had only scheduled Kevin until morning tea, as I knew he had a lot to organise in the afternoon and get ready for. The morning flew by, and it was already 10:30 a.m., so I decided to start packing up my desk for the day and finish off any last bits and pieces I had to do before I headed home. When I had finished packing up, I walked over to Kevin and wished him a great night. As I headed to the door, Kevin called out to me just as I clutched the door handle to leave, "Oh, wait! Before you go, can we go for a drive first? I need to pick up something, and I'd like your help."

I agreed and told him, "I only packed up because I thought you were going to get ready for your ball. I didn't have anything else planned to do this afternoon, so I don't mind. I was just going home."

Kevin picked up his keys from his desk, and I got my handbag. I couldn't work out what he would need my help with; he had so many people working for him … and today of all days. I had no idea what he was up too. We had been driving for about fifteen minutes in his car, heading a direction I hadn't been before with Kevin. I have always been a country girl at heart, and I literally only know how to get to work and maybe a twenty-minute parameter around the office, and that was only because of all the client visits I did with Kevin. Other than that, I am completely hopeless!

We started up a windy narrow road, and as we drove farther up the road, I noticed that the houses looked more expensive and impressive as we went along, I had no idea what Kevin had to pick up and from whom, for that matter, as he gave me no clues whatsoever. We turned left off the road we had been driving on and drove onto a tarmacked driveway. As we drove up the long hilly driveway, I could see a beautiful grand Spanish mission-style mansion in the distance. When we got closer, I noticed it had clifftop sea views. It was set on around three acres of manicured lawns and gardens, with the most beautiful views of the ocean that I think I had ever seen in my life. I had no idea who lived here, but it was amazing!

Kevin drove up to the house and followed the driveway around. He parked the car out front and looked at me, saying, "Are you coming?"

I replied, "Hell yeah." I couldn't get out of the car quickly enough. I was curious, and I didn't care, to be honest. I was so excited. I had only seen houses like this in movies or in my dreams! As I followed Kevin up to the door, I was jerking on his arm, asking, "Who lives here?"

He laughed. "You'll see in a minute!"

As we reached the door, he knocked on the door and then just walked in. I was so nervous. "You can't just walk into someone's house like that!" I said.

Once inside the front entrance of this extraordinary home, I could see staff running around frantically everywhere. They were all calling out to Kevin, saying "Mr. Jacobs" or "Sir." I felt so silly. The penny had just dropped, and I realised whose house this belonged to.

A woman wearing a white shirt and black pants walked over to Kevin. She smiled at him and said she was ready whenever he was. Kevin responded, "Hi, Monica. How are you going? This is the Ella I was telling you about! Ella, this is Monica your stylist. She is going to help you get ready today."

"Get ready for what?" I responded in a confused yet cheeky voice.

He smiled at me, and Monica said, "The ball, silly, as if you didn't know. Let's go!" She took my hand and started walking up the three-metre-wide grand luxurious staircase. Above was the most spectacular diamond-dripping chandelier hanging from the ceiling. Kevin watched me walk away from the bottom of the stairs, and I had my neck twisted and my head looking back at him the entire time I was being dragged up the staircase.

Upon reaching the top of the staircase, we walked down a long hall until we reached a room. I followed Monica, walking in behind her, unable to believe this house. It was all your dreams coming true at once, a fairy tale almost. The room we had just entered was an actual day spa/salon. "This house has everything," I said aloud.

Monica laughed and said, "Well, Kevin's a very wealthy man."

I've always felt it would be nice to own fancy things, but I had never felt the need or the desire to be surrounded by them. In saying that, I had never seen anything like this in my life. This house was magnificent. It literally astounded me! Even I could appreciate its beauty and the extraordinary architectural design and history. I realised at this point that this was how the other half lived.

She sat me down and started to remove my existing make-up and reapply my make-up. Monica told me how lucky I was to be Kevin's date to the ball.

I said, "Kevin and I aren't like that. I am married. We're just friends, and I'm his assistant." I was continuing to stress this to her as she started to do my hair.

She chuckled to herself and said, "So is Kevin ... I have done his wife's hair and make-up for years! I can tell you that you are the first woman he has ever let step foot into this house. So you must mean something to him." I sat there in silence, just thinking about what she had said as she put loose, bouncy curls through my hair and started to apply fake lashes to my eyelids. I glanced over and saw her pick up her phone and text someone. She finished applying my lashes, and I had my first look in the mirror. As corny as it sounds, I have always loved dressing up from the time I was a small girl, so when I looked in the mirror, this felt like a childhood fantasy coming to life. It didn't feel real!

I heard the door open, and Kevin walked into the room wearing a slick black suit with a black bow tie. He was so ridiculously handsome. He always had been, but I seriously believe that this man got better looking every single day. He was carrying a suit bag over his shoulder and holding a long rectangular black velvet box in his hand. He was walking towards me with a smile. He thanked Monica for her time and asked her if he could have a moment alone with me. She nodded and then left the room.

He looked me up and down, held on to the tips of my fingers, and said, "Wow, you look amazing. I mean, you always look amazing … but wow!" I blushed and continued to giggle at him. "I got something for you to wear tonight. I hope it fits," Kevin said eagerly as he held the bag by the coat hanger.

I started to unzip the bag slowly, and I got a glimpse of the dress. It was so beautiful. As I took the dress out of the bag completely, I prayed to myself that it would fit me. My hips had always been a problem as far as clothes, but I was asking everyone above for help. It was a bright red strapped backless gown with low-lying cleavage. It was so feminine and elegant; I just loved it. Never in the past had I worn a dress this revealing. I was a bit scared that there would be too much flesh showing. At the same time, I felt flattered that Kevin thought I would be able to pull off this type of dress. He told me I could go into the other room to get changed and put the dress on in private.

I went around the corner and into the other room to find Monica waiting to help me get into my dress. She was holding a pair of nude heels. I was incredibly grateful, as many people wouldn't realise how hard these gowns were to get into, and the shoes were in my size as well! I put the gown on, and Monica helped play with the dress until all the right places popped and all the other places were tucked. I was so thankful it fit!

Returning to the other room, I saw Kevin glance over at me. He held his hand to his heart and smiled ear-to-ear at me. He asked me to turn slowly around as he opened the black velvet box. I was standing in front of the mirror and watching him in the mirror as he moved my hair out of the way and gently placed a diamond necklace around my neck. He lightly tickled the back of my neck with his finger before slowly moving my hair back. I felt shivers run up my spine. He placed his hands on my waist and turned my body around by moving my hips towards him. He then stood up close to my face and said, "You know, that lipstick you're wearing matches your dress!" I nodded in agreement. "Ella Jade, will you be my date for the ball?" Kevin asked. I laughed in response. I couldn't help it—he was being so damn corny, and I felt like Cinderella before the ball.

I asked him where his wife was … and why he wasn't taking her instead of me. He replied, "She's gone away with her sister. She doesn't care for my foundation anyway. She doesn't believe in it. She thinks it's a joke and has never shown up in the past, so I stopped inviting her a long time ago. You realise, Ella, that this is the first night—if you say yes—that I would have had a date to my own ball!" I was shocked with what he had just said. But of course I agreed to be his date. I was already wearing the dress and the diamond necklace. I told him I would have to call Robbie to let him know that I had a work function that night and wouldn't be getting home until late.

I couldn't believe that his wife couldn't take it seriously, this charity ball he had started for his sister who had passed away. I so often in the past had admired wealthy couples and wondered about their lives. I had wondered if they had the same struggles as the rest of us. But I soon realised that the more money you have, the lonelier you may be.

I snuck into the other room and made a call to Robbie, letting him know that I was going to be home late. I could tell by his tone in his voice that he was rather unimpressed about it, but he still wished me a nice night and told me to be careful, and saying that he would see me when I got home. When I walked back into the room, Kevin put his arm out for me to hook mine around his, and then we started walking slowly down the staircase towards the door, making our way back to the car, which one of his staff members had just turned on to get ready for us to get in and go. The man waited by the door and then opened it for me. As I slowly slid my body across the seat, as I didn't want my dress to move the slightest, the man picked up the bottom of my gown and placed it into the car. After he gently closed my door, Kevin looked over at me and apologised to me for taking his car. He told me that he could have organised a car for us to arrive in, but he was a control freak and liked being in control of the vehicle at all times. My husband was the exact same when it came to driving, so it didn't bother me in the slightest. I told him that I preferred his car anyway; it was sexy and fast! We had a good laugh.

As we drove to the ball, we spoke about how important this annual event was to him. He told me how much he loved his sister and said that he would give anything to have her back. He explained how much she suffered and how much his parents struggled with her death. He sighed and said, "I wish every day that she didn't have to go through the pain she did." I told him I could relate to his pain, as my mother had died two years prior to a brain tumour, adding that cancer is a terrible curse and no one should ever have to suffer like that. As he drove, he smiled at me and squeezed my hand, saying "It's always the good ones who suffer."

The valet staff greeted us as soon as we arrived, opening the doors of the vehicle for us. Kevin walked around the car to my side as he rebuttoned his jacket. He held his hand out for me to take his hand to help me get out of the car. He then hooked his arm around mine and said to me with a smile on his face, "Are you ready? Don't be overwhelmed. It can be full-on! Take a deep breath and please try to have fun." As we walked up the steps together, we were greeted at the door by the event staff. They knew exactly who Kevin was and told him that they hoped the night was to his satisfaction. They then wished us both a great night. We walked through the entrance into an elegant old refurbished grand ballroom that had romantic European charm and a chic ambiance about it, with beautiful soaring ceilings, sweeping stairs, and city views.

As we walked into the room, I had a look around and noticed it was full of the elite, the rich and famous, the beautiful, and the young and old surgery-loving queens. The champagne was flowing through a sea of diamonds and gowns. I could tell straight away that everyone was curious about who I was, as I was holding on to Kevin's arm, and Kevin had never brought anyone with him in the past. It wasn't long before people were coming over to me and introducing themselves. I was struggling to try to remember all the names and where they had come from. It was extremely overwhelming. Kevin could clearly tell I was feeling anxious. He kept looking down and winking at me almost as if to say, *It's okay. I'm right here.*

I caught the eyes of an older wealthy couple from across the room. They had been watching Kevin and me mingle with the other guests for a while. I could tell they came from old money. Such people seemed to have a particular way of holding themselves, confidently and fearlessly! I would say they were in their late sixties, and she was dressed fabulously. She was wearing one of the largest diamonds I had ever seen. She had a massive rock as her engagement ring on her wedding finger. It looked vintage, and behind it was a slim detailed matching wedding band. She was wearing an elegant white slimline gown and was in great shape for her age, as was her husband. He was a very good-looking older man, and he seemed familiar to me. I just didn't know why. He was also wearing a black suit with a bow tie, as they approached she said "Kevin! Tell me, dear, who do we have here?"

"This is Ella Jade," said Kevin. He paused and looked at them and back to me with a nervous smile. "Ella, this is my mother, June, and my father." As soon as he said that, I realised that was the reason Harry looked so familiar to me. It was because Kevin had similar facial features to his father.

June gave me a mammoth smile, put one hand over her heart, and said, "So nice to meet you, dear. I have heard so much about you!" As she put her hand out to shake mine, she leaned in to me and kissed me on the cheek.

Harry put his hand out and lightly touched my hand, tilting his head to the side, and then leaned in towards me, kissing me on my cheek.

"You look so beautiful, Ella. I hope you are having fun," said June. I thanked her and told her I was. She told me she wouldn't hold us up; there was lots of fun to be had. She then leaned into Kevin to kiss him on the cheek and softly whispered in his ear, "You didn't tell me, son, that she was that beautiful."

Kevin laughed and said, "I'll catch up with you both later. I have a couple of speeches to make, and I'll come and find you when they're done." They both smiled and told me how nice it was to meet me.

The night had just begun, and it was getting off to a great start. Kevin had already raised a lot of money for his charity. I only drink a few times a year, for special occasions, normally when I meet up with my two best friends, so I was trying to be careful, as champagne goes straight to my head, but I honestly had no choice. I just couldn't help it! I would be slowly sipping on my drink, and as soon as I finished it, I would pop my glass down on one of the tables behind me and someone would immediately put another glass in my hand. It was terrible. You didn't even realise you were doing it. If you hold a drink long enough, you end up drinking it.

Kevin kept being dragged away from me to entertain his other guests; I was on my own. I suppose I wasn't, as I was Kevin's date. Many people were talking to me throughout the night and asking me endless questions about Kevin's and my relationship. I told everyone that asked that I was Kevin's personal assistant and not his date, not that anyone I spoke to believed me. I had been talking so much my mouth was getting terribly dry. I was trying to be so careful with my drinks, as this was my employer's event after all, and I didn't want to get drunk and embarrass myself, or him, but I had to keep having sips of my drink just to put some liquid in my mouth to stop it drying out. I started to feel very happy and slightly tipsy. I hadn't eaten anything yet, as all the food floating around the room by the waitstaff was meat and pastry, the two types of foods I cannot eat.

Kevin came over to me, put his hand through my arm, and rested that hand on my lower back, whispering in my ear, "I am just checking you are having a nice night. I'm sorry I keep getting dragged away from you! I know you are quite capable of taking care of yourself, considering your track record. I knew you would be fine, and you also understand my role for this evening. May I say … I love it when you wear that colour?" He gave me a cheeky smile as he nudged his hip against mine.

I laughed and asked him, "When have you seen me wear anything other than black!"

He leaned back into my ear and whispered, "I've seen you in a similar colour before, and I don't think I'll ever be able to erase that image from my brain, and I don't think I ever want to either, to be honest!" I couldn't help but giggle. He was referring to the time I stripped off to my underwear for the meeting.

He said, "You must be starving, Ella!" He put his hand up in the air and attracted one of the waitstaff. When the young woman came over to us, Kevin told her he had arranged a special meal to be put aside for him. The woman nodded and told us she would be right back. Kevin looked over and winked at me with a proud smile. The woman came back with a plate of vegan gluten-free healthy finger food for me. She handed me the plate, and I was so relieved and excited, for I could eat everything on this plate. I looked over at Kevin and kissed him on his cheek, thanking him for being so wonderful to me. The expression on Kevin's face when he saw my reaction to the food was as if he got off on pleasing me and seeing me happy. It was so strange.

As we were standing together side by side, slow music began to play and couples started making their way over to the dance floor. I had just finished my food and stood there in awe, just watching them dance. Kevin could see me watching them and asked me if I would like to dance with him. I took his hand, and we began to slow dance. We danced a few songs together, and I could hear people talking about us, but in that moment, I didn't care. We were having so much fun, and that's all that mattered.

Time got away from us; the night had flown. At 11:30 p.m., the music volume came down and the lights began to get slightly brighter until coming to full brightness. A man came over the speaker and said, "Thank you all for a great night! I'd like to drag Kevin Jacobs up here for one last time. We hope you all continue to have a fantastic night!"

The spotlight hit us both, and everyone was looking at us. Kevin squeezed my hand and said, "I'll be right back."

He walked onto the stage, took the microphone from the presenter, and said, "Thank you all so much for dressing up. Ladies, you all look beautiful! Gents, you don't look too shabby yourselves! I would like to thank you all for the annual support you give this foundation—you all know how much this means to me and my amazing parents, June and Harry. The count has been done, and we have raised just over ten million dollars, more than last year! Everyone, please raise your glasses ... I couldn't be more grateful for all your generosity. I thank you all and wish you a great night and a safe drive home. There's still plenty of food and alcohol, and the music doesn't turn off until one a.m., so … cheers to all!"

Kevin passed the microphone back to the presenter. When he got off the edge of the stage, there were a couple of women waiting there for him. They grabbed him by his arms, trying to get his attention. They then tried to drag him to the dance floor to dance with them! They were attractive girls but had a trashy, loose look to them. I could see him from across the room trying to escape. I thought it was incredibly funny and giggled at him. He certainly would never have any trouble picking up—they came to him! He managed to escape from their claws and paws, and then he came and found me.

The lights dimmed, and the music volume went back up. That's when the actual party started! Eighties party classics began to play, and everyone made a mad dash to the dance floor. They were all dancing and jumping around, having a great time. I was really starting to feel the alcohol and was loving life! Kevin took photos of us and the people we were dancing with. We were pulling funny faces for the camera. He put his phone back in his jacket pocket and then started to dance close to me.

At one, the lights came back on fully and the music slowly came to a stop. I felt disappointed, as I didn't want the night to end. I was having so much fun and didn't want to go home, not yet, anyway. Kevin told me that due to noise restrictions, the venue had to begin wrapping things up at one. He took hold of both my hands and looked into my eyes, asking me if I wanted to go anywhere else or if I was ready to go home. I took a deep breath, thanked him for a wonderful night, and told him I'd best be on my way home. I didn't really want to go home, but I felt it was my safest option.

He then asked me if I wanted him to take me home, and I told him I would be fine catching a taxi. He tried to fight me on it, and I could tell he was worried about it. But I told him I would message him as soon as I walked into the house. He seemed less tense about that idea and then ordered me a taxi. We walked out the front, and he leaned into me, kissed me slowly and softly on my left cheek, lightly grabbed the back of my hair, and squeezed me into his chest for a goodbye hug. He told me he wished I didn't have to go home. I agreed and stepped back, away from him, and walked towards the taxi. The driver got out and opened the back driver's side door for me. I got into the car and looked back at Kevin. He had not taken his eyes off me the entire time.

On the drive home in the taxi I realised, thinking back, how many times in a day Kevin touched me in general and how I had never even flinched! I should, but I didn't. I could tell he didn't want me to leave—well, not to go home to Robbie, anyway! Part of me felt bad leaving him there, but I had to get home. I felt I was already going to be in the bad books, and I wasn't adding adultery to the mix.

It took around an hour to get home from the venue. I had been messaging Kevin along the way, as he was concerned for my safety, dressed up and alone in the taxi. I did understand why he was stressed out, which is why I texted him along the way, until I arrived in the driveway, and then I said my final goodnight.

Chapter 7

Contoured Cheekbone

I WALKED INTO the house and through to the kitchen, placing my purse and phone on the kitchen counter, and continuing to walk into our lounge. I noticed Robbie sitting in the corner couch in the dark sipping on vodka on ice, holding his phone, and facing right in my direction. I could tell by the look on his face that I was in deep shit. My heart started racing, and my hand started to tremble as he stood up and said, "Did you have fun, baby?" He waved the phone in my direction sarcastically. He did it so quickly that I could only just get a glimpse of what he was on about. It was a photo of Kevin and me from the Ball. Kevin must have uploaded the photo and tagged my name to it on his Facebook after I left the party. "Huh! Answer me, you fucking whore! Did you have fun with your boyfriend?"

I had seen that look of rage before, just not by him! I didn't know what else to do; I just ran straight to the bathroom and locked the door behind me. He chased me and started bashing the door and screaming. "Ella Jade, open this fucking door! I swear, Ella … The longer you are in there, the worse it will be!" I just sat on the floor holding the door with my back, resting my head up against it, praying it wouldn't open. As I sat there feeling the vibrations through the door from his punching and kicking the door in rage, I wasn't crying. I didn't even feel emotional! I had never seen my husband get to this level. I had experienced it in the past with my father and other jealous men I had previously dated, just not with Robbie! I was waiting for him to get all of his rage out, and then I was hoping he would calm down and go back to normal. He kicked and punched the door for a good ten minutes, and then all of a sudden … he just stopped. Nothing. Silence. My heart kicked into overdrive! The silence had me more concerned than when he was kicking and punching the door trying to get me.

I was sitting there on our cold tiled bathroom floor with a thousand thoughts racing through my mind, trying to figure out what had taken my drunk-arse husband's attention. I tried to listen through the door to hear what he was doing. I couldn't really hear anything. About a minute later, I could faintly hear him talking to someone. Who could he be talking to? I looked down and realised … "Fuck!" I said to myself in a panic. I remembered that my phone was on the kitchen counter. The prick had my phone! He knew how important my phone was to me; it was my work bible! I couldn't have him call Kevin or any of Kevin's clients.

Adrenaline rushing through my body, I bolted out of the bathroom towards the kitchen. He was standing there with a dirty, sarcastic look upon his face. He could see how fearful I was about the phone. He had been pretending to call someone on my phone to lure me out of the bathroom. He slammed my phone down on the counter and walked over to me. I could smell him from a mile away, and he stunk like a bar—vodka, beer, and cigarettes. He was in such a rage, staring at me and grinding his teeth uncontrollably. He kept asking me if I had

had fun, and I refused to answer him. He slapped his ring finger against my face with such force that I could feel it immediately start swelling and burning. I could feel a pulsing beat through my skin. I put my hands on my cheeks in shock and held them there. He then pushed me up against the wall and squeezed my face with such force that I felt as if my head were in a vice. My feet couldn't even reach the floor, as he had my face pinned against the wall and was holding my body off the ground, my toes were dangling in mid-air.

He took one hand off my face and grabbed my lips hard, holding them in a clamped pinch. I kept trying to push him off me with one hand and release his grip from my face with my other hand, but he was too strong for me. I tried to beg him to stop, trying to tell him he was hurting me, but it was just muffled cries and he didn't care. He told me, "If I find out you've fucked this Kevin—or anyone else—I will kill you! You are my wife; I fucking own you! So don't try to run—I will find you." He abruptly let go of my face, and my feet landed back on ground. He slightly leaned back and then vulgarly spat on the ground next to where my feet were. "Clean yourself up! You look fucking disgusting!" He then punched the wall above my head and stumbled outside for a cigarette.

As soon as he left, I grabbed my phone off the counter and went straight to the freezer for a bag of frozen peas. I was trying to stop the swelling as fast as I could. It wasn't the first time a man had laid hands on me, but it was the first time my Robbie had! I went back into the bathroom with my phone and the bag of peas and locked the door behind me. I turned the shower on, then took off my dress and underwear. I got into the shower with my bag of peas. I stood there with my head tilted back, letting the water hit my forehead and run down my front as I held the frozen peas against my cheekbone. I stood there in the same position for at least ten minutes.

I had so many thoughts running through my mind. The main thought I had, which I just couldn't shake, was how my husband, who always seemed so calm, the man I had never seen snap, had finally snapped! He had a look in his eyes I had never seen before. As I pulled off my artificial eyelashes and washed my body, I realised he had always been that man, the man I had seen tonight. All those past images started to flash through my mind. He had always been controlling and possessive over me, but the aggression tonight was at a whole other level. I realised I had never noticed it because I had been living in a bubble this whole time. As I had played his game to his specific needs, he had never needed to get upset. I did everything he wanted—I was his perfect woman—and the past months I was starting to slip. He had started to crack and finally show his true colours.

I got out of the shower, dried myself off, and then picked up my phone. I had a quick look on my Facebook account to see the photo that had made Robbie so furious and come at me with such force and anger. I tapped on my Facebook app and opened my account. I had a notification that I had been tagged in a photo, and I had a heap of notifications letting me know that many people had liked the photo. I clicked on the photo I had been tagged in, and it was Kevin and me, drunk on the dance floor, pulling funny faces. It really wasn't a big deal—it was quite innocent and humorous. I could see why Kevin saw no harm in putting the photo on Facebook. At this point, I realised Robbie was seriously out of control!

I unlocked the door and walked out into the hallway. I couldn't see Robbie anywhere. I went into our bedroom and walked into our walk-in wardrobe. Turning the light on, I looked back into our bedroom and I could see Robbie asleep in our bed. I stood there and watched him as he slept for a moment, thinking, *Am I scared of my husband, the man I didn't realise he had always been? No! I am not afraid of him, but I am now well aware of him and what he truly is capable of.* I went to my clothes drawers, placed my towel on top, and pulled out a nighty and fresh underwear. I put them on and then turned out the light of our wardrobe, crawling into bed next to my drunken husband. It took me a while, but I did finally fall asleep.

I woke up that next morning to Robbie's work alarm. He pressed the snooze button, and I just lay there until he got out of bed. I could still feel my face aching. It didn't surprise me that morning that he woke up like normal for work. He was slightly more hung-over than usual, but he still got up for work. As usual, I helped him get ready. He kissed me goodbye, grabbed hold of my hand on his way out, and told me he would see me tonight as he walked to the front door. I nodded. As soon as I watched his car leave our driveway, I went straight into our bedroom and changed into my running gear. I needed to go for a run so badly. It was still dark outside, as it was early in the morning. Running was something that I did for myself, and it made me feel free. I could be anyone I wanted to be.

I ran for a good hour and tried to get last night out of my head. I had had such a wonderful evening with Kevin, and then it took a turn for the worse with Robbie! I got back home covered in sweat before the sun had come up and jumped straight into the shower. I pumped up the music in the bathroom and screamed out the lyrics as I washed the sweat off my body. I got out of the shower and dried myself off. Once I was completely dry, I just stood there, naked in the mirror, just looking at myself—at the bruised face woman looking back at me! I started heavily applying concealer to my cheekbone. I thought, *If he had hit me a centimetre lower, it wouldn't have looked so bad.* Then I realised my chin was all bruised from when he had been holding me by my face off the ground. The lighting was dull in our bathroom, and I hadn't noticed it before. As I tried to cover my chin with concealer before work, I spoke to myself aloud: "Why do all men seem to think they can mistreat me, use me, and abuse me? Robbie has always been my safe choice ... until now!"

Arriving at work, I was trying to look and act completely normal as I headed into the office, past Heather, then into the office I shared with Kevin. I could tell how I looked. I could feel my swollen cheek and the throbbing pain coming out through my skin. I had no other words to describe how I felt emotionally in that moment other than ... *numb*. I said good morning to Kevin as he was taking a sip of his coffee. He started to say good morning but only said, "Ella!" I could see the shocked look on his face. He immediately stopped drinking and put the cup straight down onto his desk. Kevin took one look at me and clearly knew the kind of night I had. This man could see into my soul somehow. I was not sure how he did it, but he just did.

I sat down at my desk, put my handbag underneath it, and took out my phone before turning on my computer to get my day started. As I placed my phone on the desk, Kevin asked me to cancel all meetings for the day, as he didn't want to see anyone today. I called every single client and cancelled all meetings for the day as he had requested, rescheduling them for the next week. I let him know that his day was now free, and then I started to catch up on paperwork I had previously pushed aside.

As I was working away, my phone vibrated on my desk. I looked over and could see I had received a text message from Robbie: "How is your day going? Did you end up going to work today? I'm sorry for last night, Ella. I'm not sure what came over me! I really hope you can forgive me. XXX." I replied: "My day is good so far. Don't stress about it. Everything is good. I am at work. I'll see you tonight when I get home. XX."

I put my phone down and took a deep breath, picked up a small pile of paperwork with one hand, and stood up to walk over to the filing cabinets on the wall to file the documents.

Kevin instantly got out of his chair and started to move towards me. He had been watching me all morning, staring at me and flicking his pen on his paperwork on his desk. I could tell he wanted to talk to me but was unsure what to do. As I headed across the room, Kevin grabbed me by my hand and forced me to a stop. I turned my body to look at him, and he gently took hold of my face, leaning his face into mine, and started to kiss me softly over my over-concealed bruised cheekbone. He then slowly moved his kisses down my neck. I loosened the grip in my hand, and the paperwork dropped to the ground. It got my attention, and I asked him to stop. He slowly pulled away from my neck and just looked down into my eyes. I couldn't move my body. I was utterly powerless—I am not sure why, but I had uncontrollable word vomit and just blurted it out: "Kevin, everyone makes mistakes! I don't want to be yours!"

He gently held on to my face and looked into my eyes. "I promise I will never hurt you, Ella!" He tilted his head and moved his hand behind my ear, lightly massaging my skin and tickling my hair as his fingers softly touched my hair, slightly moving it. He began to kiss my lips, and his touch was so gentle and genuine. He slowly moved down to my neck and kissed me there. He then pushed my hair out of his way.

I only had a few thoughts going through my mind. The truth was that I didn't really want him to stop. It felt so good, and I knew it was wrong, but it didn't really feel wrong. It felt so natural, and I just couldn't help myself. I didn't want him to stop. I started to undo the buttons on his shirt and run my fingers down his firmly toned abs. As he kissed my neck, I pushed his shirt off his shoulders and pulled the back of his shirt until both of his hands were free and he was topless. I noticed all the tattoos across his body; I didn't even realise he had them! I followed them with my fingers from his chest to his shoulder and around to his back.

He slowly pushed me up against the wall where I was standing and continued to kiss the other side of my neck. I closed my eyes and tilted my head, leaning it against the wall. I was loving how he was touching me, and I had these incredible sensations flowing through my body. I heard him undo his belt and unzip his suit pants. He slowly lifted up my dress, and his fingers moved my lace underwear to the side. He slid his penis inside me, squeezing my arse cheeks together as he thrust his body against mine. I rolled my head back and started to look at the ceiling. I was enjoying him inside me as he continued to kiss my neck and pull my hair tightly. It felt incredible! I didn't want it to stop. This man really knew how to hit every button I had in me. I couldn't contain myself. My moans got louder and louder until I reached the pinnacle of orgasms. My body was trembling, and I couldn't hold my legs up properly. I opened my eyes and could see him slightly leaning back, mouth open, breathing heavily, and his body slightly jolting, with his eyes rolling back into his head. He had come. I couldn't help but laugh as I was trying to regain my balance. I had never experienced anything like that in my life.

He put both hands on the wall, resting them above my head where I was leaning. I could see his biceps tense and get bigger. He smiled and told me he had wanted to do that to me for so long. He slowly kissed me one more time on my swollen cheekbone, then took himself out of me and started to do up his pants. He asked me if I would like it if he got some food and wine delivered to the office and we could just spend the day together. I told him I would love that. We sat down on the couch together and promised each other from that moment, we would not mention our partners for the day. It was our day to spend together.

We spent the rest of the day snuggled up together on the couch in our office, drinking wine and eating naughty treats from the local cafe. It was so romantic and relaxing. I thought that after we had had sex, our relationship might change—when a man gets what he wants, it normally comes to an end—but with Kevin it actually felt as if it only became deeper. I felt as if we were one. It was always so easy with him.

At the end of the day, I was so relieved that the top floor of our building had a private shower in the bathroom. If I had gone home smelling like another man, I really would be dead! As soon as I walked out of our office towards the main bathroom to have a shower, Heather began throwing filthy looks towards me. I couldn't help but laugh, as I realised she must have heard us. She had been Kevin's receptionist for the past four years—and nothing had ever happened between the two of them. I could tell that she was enraged with jealously.

I went into the bathroom and had a shower, redid my make-up, and headed back to our office. It was six, so I had to be leaving. I grabbed my handbag and phone, and Kevin got up off the couch and walked me to the door. We both stood there at the closed door. He smiled, looking down at me as I looked up at him. He held on to my face and lightly massaged my cheek, kissing me three times softly on my lips. As he pulled his face away from mine, he said in a nervous voice, "Call me if you need anything, Ella Jade, please. I will get there as soon as I can!"

I smiled and leaned towards him for one more kiss, reassuring him that everything would be fine and that I would see him tomorrow. I made my way to my car and headed home. I called Robbie on my way and asked if he needed anything from the shops. I bought a couple of items and continued on my way home.

That night, I made dinner as usual. Robbie had helped me set the table, which he had never previously done. We ate dinner, and I then washed up and got ready for bed. I could tell from the moment I walked into our house that Robbie wanted to talk to me, to try to smooth things over from the night before. I think he realised he had gone too far. The problem was that I had reached the point where I didn't even care enough to try to fix it. I do believe he realised that as well. I would honestly take partial reasonability for his getting upset, as the whole night, I was treated like Kevin's date and not his employee, but I refused to take full ownership of his outburst. Robbie only saw one photo that had been uploaded to Facebook, and it was quite an innocent photo for him to get so out of control. I knew I could never trust his temper again. The worst part was that I ended up doing what he feared most—and I didn't feel any remorse in doing so! Sleeping with Kevin felt so incredible. Not one part of me felt guilty about it. I thought it was crazy because I should feel guilty about committing adultery, but being with Kevin felt more natural than when I made love to Robbie.

The next day, as soon as the office door closed, Kevin was standing in the entrance of the door waiting for me! He didn't say a word. He just took me by the waist and picked me up. I wrapped my legs around his waist as he was passionately kissing my lips. He held my body aloft and pushed my back up against the wall, my legs still wrapped around him. As we were kissing, I looked down at him, holding on to his chin, massaging his facial hair on his lower cheek. We were now moving along the wall, hitting the picture frames and making them fall off their hooks and crash and smash to the ground. We both looked at all the broken pictures on the floor and began to laugh.

He walked me over to his desk, holding me with one hand and using his other hand to push everything off his desk and to the floor. He sat me on the corner of his desk and pulled my dress over my head. He started to rush and undo his belt, saying, "I couldn't sleep last night. I couldn't get you out of my head!" He took off his shirt and threw it to the floor, starting to kiss my neck. I tilted my head as he kissed and lightly breathed on my neck, playing with my hair—when all of a sudden we heard the door sound.

We looked at each and said simultaneously, "Breakfast!"

I grabbed his shirt, threw it over me, and quickly hid behind the door. He walked over to the door laughing, as he was topless. I had stolen his shirt, and his pants were partially open, with his belt just clinging to his pants. He opened the door and let the café deliveryman walk into the room and put our breakfast on Kevin's desk. I continued to hide behind the door wearing Kevin's shirt, hiding my nude lace push-up underwear set. As the deliveryman left, Kevin thanked him and then locked the door behind him. I couldn't help but laugh at him.

He took the back of my neck with one hand and pulled my face into his, saying, "Come here, you!" We started kissing each other passionately as we giggled. He picked me up and took me over to his desk, moving the food out of the way and placing me down on the edge of the desk again. He took his shirt off me and unclipped the back of my bra, removing it by sliding it over my arms. He leaned down and took my breasts in both his hands, putting them up to his mouth and starting to kiss and softly suck on my nipples. I held on to his face and tilted my head back, closing my eyes. It felt so good.

He then went down to his knees and put his hands underneath my bum. He slightly lifted me up and removed my underwear. Then he slowly pulled them down my legs and over my feet. He pushed my legs open, holding my inner thighs, lifting them and placing them down on his shoulders, resting my feet on his back. He started slowly kissing my vagina and slowly moving his tongue up and down while he was still kissing me at the same time. I leant my body and head back on the desk and used one of my arms to hold on to the desk, holding my body weight, and then used the other to massage his face as he continued to go down on me. My moans get louder, and I squeezed my inner knees to his face as the feelings increased. I didn't want him to stop. This man really knew how to please a woman. It didn't take long for me at all. I felt as if I were going to explode from inside. I held the back of his head down, running my fingers through his hair as my body spasmed. I could feel tingles rushing through my body, and I cried out a long final moan. He looked up at me as I bit my lips, still enjoying the tingling rush I felt consuming my body. He laughed and sat back up. "You really enjoyed that!"

"Mmm," I replied as I nodded and grinned. I was still my finding my words. I put my legs down and sat on the edge of the desk, gripping both his hands and pulling him up to stand. He leaned down, and I kissed him on the lips and then slid my bottom off the desk and got down to my knees. I unzipped his pants and slid them down his legs, then the same for his cotton briefs, until they were both free over his feet. I started to kiss his penis slowly, running my tongue from the bottom until I reached the tip. When I put it into my mouth, he grabbed my hair and started moving my head back and forth. As I kept going, his moans got louder.

He looked down at me and said, "I'm not going to last long if you keep doing what you're doing right now!"

I looked up at him, smiled, and kept going. He squeezed the back of my hair tightly and leaned his head back. With his mouth open, he started to slightly jolt as he gave three strong final thrusts into my mouth, and I knew he had just finished. He moved his hand to my chin and lightly rubbed it with his thumb, smiling down at me and biting his lower lip. He pulled me up to standing and held our naked bodies together, hugging me and kissing my neck. I asked him, "Are you ready for breakfast, hot stuff?"

He replied, "We just ate!" As he laughed and tickled my lower back while joking around, I couldn't help but laugh and shake my head at him. I went around the desk to my breakfast, picked up my smoothie, and quickly washed down the taste I still had in my mouth. I sat down on his chair at his desk, eating my breakfast as he leaned against the desk facing me, smiling at me as we ate our breakfast.

After I finished eating, I jumped out of his seat and said, "Oh, shit! We have to get dressed, Kevin. We have an eight thirty appointment with Joe at his office! It will take us at least twenty minutes to drive there! *We have to get ready and go!*" I stressed to him as I picked up his shirt off the floor and passed it to him.

He laughed and said, "Relax. I've already cancelled all our appointments this morning and moved them to this afternoon."

I was shocked! "You did?" I asked him, amused as I pictured him quickly calling everyone before I arrived this morning.

"I wanted to spend more time with you this morning. I was craving you all night! I seriously haven't slept," he told me as he played with my hair.

"In that case ... round two!" I said. I slid on his shirt, which I was holding over my naked body, dancing around in it, and his face lit up and he nodded.

"My shirt looks so much better on you! I love it ... So sexy, Ella! Come here." He played with the bottom of his shirt, leaning down and rocking me side to side. He then picked me up and laid me flat on my back on the carpet. We started to mess around, almost play fighting, when I rolled on top of him. I'm not sure why I did it. As soon as I did, I realised that I hated this position. I don't know how, but he noticed something was off. He sat up to an almost sitting position instantly. "It's okay—I'm right here!" he said as he started to softly kiss my lips and gently pinch my chin.

The feelings of insecurity instantly left my body, and I smiled, starting to thrust back and forth on top of him as he held on to and kissed my breasts. I felt so alive. He understood my body and mind, and it was the first time in my life I felt as if I had actually made love to someone. I thrust back and forth until I cried out the loudest moan and had the best orgasm I think I had ever had.

He squeezed my breasts hard and then jolted his pelvis. He fell flat on his back with a smile on his face. "My God, girl. I think you're going to kill me!"

I laughed and said, "Again!" He smiled weakly and put his hand around my neck, pulling me to his chest and snuggling my head underneath his chin. We lay there in each other's arms for around ten minutes. Time went so quickly that I could have stayed in that moment for the rest of my life.

Over the next week, we had sex every day in every position known. We managed to have sex on every piece of furniture in our office! One day, we were in such a mad rush after a meeting to be with one another that I jumped on top of him in his car in the car park. Luckily, he had dark tinted windows and no one could see me bouncing up and down topless on top of him. He told me after we had finished that he had never had sex in his car before and that he loved it.

On Friday night, as I was leaving for the weekend, he said that he loved being with me and that he had images pressed into his mind of him doing me from behind in the bathroom, up against the mirror. He told me he loved that position, as he liked watching my facial expressions from behind as I orgasmed. He told me that those images were ingrained in his mind and it was the only thing that would get him through the weekend. I giggled, and he gave me three slow kisses on the lips, pinching my arse cheek as I started to walk away. I slightly turned to look back at him as he was standing there watching me walk away, slightly biting his bottom lip.

CHAPTER 8

$\mathcal{I}$ Want a Baby

IT WAS ROBBIE'S birthday. Today he turned thirty-four years old. I had contacted his family last week and organised a dinner party at our house for him. His parents and two siblings were able to make it, but his older brother couldn't make it, as he had to work. I'd spoken to Kevin and asked him if I could leave a couple of hours earlier to prepare for the dinner party. He didn't mind at all; he just told me that he was shattered that he'd missed out on the couple of hours with me. Then he said with a laugh, "This once off, Ella, will be fine, and you will have to make it up to me next week … by doing that thing I like!" I agreed, retrieved my bag, kissed him goodbye, and thanked him.

I stopped on my way home and bought some fresh produce for dinner and dessert. As soon as I got home, I started to prepare dinner. I made dessert first, apple and pear crumble, which was my mother's famous recipe. I could make it with my eyes closed. I quickly whipped it up and popped it into the fridge out of my way so I could get started on making dinner. I was cooking chicken Thai curry. I loved cooking dishes like this—all I had to do was serve mine up first, then add the chicken to the curry afterwards and I had both his and my vegetarian dishes done. I always made sure that when I cooked for his family, I ate the same-looking food, as they could be most critical of me and my dietary requirements. Robbie got embarrassed about my eating habits and never stood up for me to his family! His father thought there was something wrong with me, and his mother was always telling me I was too skinny and would need to get used to eating meat, as one day I would be pregnant with her grandchild—saying that if I didn't eat meat, it would harm my baby! Truly intelligent people … not!! I just smile and agree in order to keep the peace. It's not worth the fight.

I finished getting dinner on and left it on low to simmer. In the meantime, I put together an antipasto cheese platter and got the wine and glasses ready for when they walked in the door. I looked at the time. They were expected in around twenty minutes, so I went to the bedroom and changed into a nice dinner dress, also touching up my make-up in the bathroom. I heard Robbie walk in the front door, and he walked straight into the bedroom. He grabbed the clothes I had just laid on the end of the bed for him, and he then gave me a greeting kiss and continued to walk straight to the bathroom to have a shower.

Heading out to the kitchen while I waited for them to arrive, I poured myself a glass of red wine, taking sips from my wine as well as a deep breath. I really needed this. As I enjoyed every sip, I thought before they all arrived how I always got nervous before his family came over. I just found them so loud and aggressive. His mother was always trying to pluck information from me. It was horrible. I was a private person, and they just didn't understand that. They made me feel as I'm a snob, which is not the case. I would just rather listen than talk, especially talk about myself—it's just who I am!

Robbie got out of the shower, dressed, and did his hair. He came into the kitchen, and I wished him a happy birthday, telling him he had to come out to the garage for me to give him his present. He looked very happy, even though he hates surprises, he followed me outside. We walked into the garage, and he saw a huge rectangular box with a big blue bow on it. He smiled and put his hands together, saying, "Hmm, I wonder what it is." He went over to the present and started to unwrap it. As the newspaper ripped away, his smile got wider. Once he got all the gift wrapping off, he came over and gave me a kiss, thanking me. "You even got the colour right, Ella" he said. I had bought him a bright green Kincrome toolbox. I knew he needed one, so I was happy.

I heard car doors sound from the driveway and told Robbie his family must have arrived. We walked out of the garage, and I could see his parents. I smiled in their direction as we both went over to them. I gave them each a greeting kiss on the cheek, and then they both hugged Robbie and wished him a happy birthday, handing him his gifts. I suggested to Robbie that he open his gifts inside so he could sit down and so I could get everyone a glass of wine. He agreed, and we headed inside to the kitchen. Robbie sat down at our kitchen counter and started unwrapping his presents as I poured each of his parents a glass of wine. His sister and brother-in-law had just arrived, and we greeted them. Then I poured them each a glass of wine.

I always try to get away quickly from his sister's husband Tony. The man creeps me out. He was the only one in the family who ever hugged me, or even liked me, but it was never a quick hello hug. It was a slow, inappropriate hug, and he always tried to push my breasts up against his chest. It was so disgusting. He did it every time, and no one ever noticed! After getting everyone a drink, I stood back in my kitchen, watching them all hover around the kitchen counter, where the cheese and dips were, simply watching as they were all eating, chatting, and talking over one another. Tony came over to me and asked me how I was going. I always deflected the conversation to him. It was easy, as he was so full of himself. He loved talking about himself, and he didn't even notice I did it. I asked everyone how long until they would like me to serve up dinner. I turned the oven on to heat up, as it took a good forty minutes to bake my crumble so it would be ready to eat after we had finished dinner.

I served dinner, and we all sat down at our dining table to eat. We all raised our glasses to Robbie and wished him a happy birthday. I take a sip of my wine and then started to eat. His sister began talking over dinner about all the updates with the family and friends circle. She said that their cousin who got married last year was now officially three months pregnant and expecting their first child. Everyone was happy and excited for them, and it was not long before someone said it: "So, Ella, when do you think you and Robbie will start trying?" It was his father, John.

I took a sip of my wine and nervously replied, "I'm not sure. I'm not really ready yet!"

"Ready for what, Ella!" asked his mother with a tone to her voice.

"I have a great job, and I am just not mentally ready for a baby right now."

"You're never mentally ready for a screaming baby—you just deal with it!" his mother told me. I looked over at Robbie and saw him shaking his head at me.

"Robbie really wants a baby, Ella. It's not fair to him, and you're holding him back!" his sister Sarah told me.

Robbie drank the rest of his wine and said, "You have to have sex to make a baby!"

They all twisted their necks around to face me, staring at me in shock. His brother in-law was looking very happy as he stared at me.

I looked over at Robbie, unable to believe he'd said that as we were eating dinner in front of his family. I felt like saying to Robbie, "Really, missionary man! Maybe if you knew how to satisfy me, I would be more eager to have sex with you." See how he liked those apples! But it really wasn't dinner or family conversation. It made me feel uncomfortable, and I felt it was unnecessary. Dinner was quickly becoming awkward! I thought, *I certainly don't want to have sex with you now, you jack arse!*

I asked if anyone needed wine topped up and got up from the table, going into the kitchen to hide for a moment. I took a deep breath to get the courage to go back out there and face the tribe. I picked up the wine and decided to drink a bit of it out of the bottle, as no one could see me. Tony walked around the corner, and I immediately pulled the bottle away from my mouth. He burst into laughter. "Wow, you already have the mum thing down pat. I see my wife doing that all the time!" I couldn't help but laugh. As much as he drove me crazy, he could always make me laugh. He obviously felt bad and was trying to cheer me up.

I passed him the bottle I had been drinking out of and opened a fresh bottle to set on the table. As we walked back out to the table, Tony whispered to me, "You know, Ella, if you ever get lonely, you know you can call me!" I just looked at him, shook my head, and told him no.

Joining the others, I saw Robbie's sister and mother whispering to Robbie, asking him questions about our sex life. When I sat back down, everyone looked at me. I took a gulp of my drink and gently cleared my throat to get everyone's attention. "I would like to add to Robbie's comment! Considering there is nothing off limits to your family, I would like to say that we do have sex. I refuse to stop taking the pill! I am not ready. If your son wants a baby so much, I'll leave and he can find someone else who does!" I sat back in my chair, and the whole room went silent.

Hearing the buzzer to the oven from the kitchen, I stood up and said, "Who's ready for dessert!" I got up and walked into the kitchen.

Robbie flew into the kitchen after me, grabbed me by my arm, and started squeezing it. "How dare you say that to my family? You can't just leave me! And you will have my baby!" he demanded.

"I'm not ready, Robbie. I don't know how many times I have to tell you!"

"What's wrong with you? Why won't you just have my baby? Why do you keep fighting me on this?"

"Because, Robbie, it's a baby, a human! It's not a dog that you decide is too hard and you can drop it off at a pound. You're a man—you can walk off and leave. Ah, but me … I'm stuck with it. I'm not ready, so why should I be forced into something so life changing!" I screamed at him. "I think that when it's the right time, I will realise I am ready. I'm thirty-one years old, not forty. I still have time! You need to stop hounding me on this subject. It's your birthday, and you should be enjoying that. Are you truly ready for twenty-four hours a day of crying, screaming, and poo? I'm not! All I meant to say was that I don't want to hold you back, if that's what you really want right now. I am sorry, but I cannot give that to you. You will have to find someone else who can," I said in a calmer voice.

"Maybe once you fall pregnant, you will feel the love for the child!" he told me in his desperation.

His mother entered the kitchen. "Look, Ella, I know you're not ready. I fear you never will be. Why don't you just go off the pill, and if and when you fall pregnant, it was meant to be!"

"That's not a bad idea," said Robbie. He looked over at me and begged, "Ella, please, what do you think!"

"Sure … Why not?" I responded sarcastically. I asked for a moment alone with Robbie. His mother rolled her eyes and left the room. I smiled at him, and he kissed me on the lips. "I will stop taking my pill. It will take a few months to come into effect, Robbie, and when it happens, it happens, no trying or planning."

He agreed, so happy that he started kissing me on my lips, and then he was trying to push me up against the bench in the kitchen. As he was kissing me, I felt him slip his tongue in my mouth. I started to get nervous; he was getting pretty hot and heavy considering his family was sitting in the next room. He slid his hands under my dress and held on to my arse under my dress as he continued to kiss me. I put my fingers in between our lips, trying to separate them so he would stop kissing me. He just moved his kisses to my neck. I told him we had to stop, that his family was in the next room, but he seriously didn't care. He started playing with my underwear, and I couldn't help but giggle. "Robbie, stop. Your mum is there! Please …," I begged him.

"Wow, people! Sudden change of heart; you're making one right now," Tony said as he walked into the kitchen, looking stunned.

Robbie pulled down my dress and covered me with his body, protecting me from Tony's eyes. He kissed me one more time and whispered to me, "To be continued." As he pinched my arse before heading back into the dining area with his family, I asked them both to bring in all the plates from dinner and I would start serving up dessert. I got the ice cream out of the freezer and popped it onto the bench to defrost for a bit while I cut up the crumble. I sliced the crumble, put the ice cream on top, and walked back into the dining room holding a couple bowls of dessert.

The atmosphere had completely changed. His mother was actually smiling at me. I put a bowl in front of everyone and sat down in my chair. "That's great, dear. We're all very happy that you're taking the first step!" She had the biggest grin on her face; it was borderline scary. I knew she was happy because she felt she had solved all our problems with one fell swoop.

Robbie leaned into me and put his arm on my shoulder, kissing me on the cheek. He winked at me and whispered in my ear, "As soon as they go, that dress is off!" My heart sank instantly. I tried to smile at him, but I had so many feelings and thoughts rushing around my head.

As we finished dessert, conversation was considerably normal considering what had happened only thirty minutes prior. Robbie stood up and thanked everyone for making it over to see him for his birthday. He started to walk his family to the door. We said our goodbyes, and they left for the evening. As soon as Robbie had closed the front door, he rushed into the kitchen and picked up my handbag from underneath the bench. He looked at me and said, "You know what you need to do?" I went over to him, reached into my handbag, and pulled out my pill prescription. I walked over to the bin and threw the pills into it. He gave me a smile of joy and approached me, starting to kiss me. He put his hands up my dress and lifted me by my arse onto the bench. He rolled up the bottom of my dress and moved it out of his way and then slid off my underwear and spread my thighs. He started to unbuckle his belt, unzipping his zipper and pulling his penis out. He slid himself into me and started thrusting in and out, softly kissing my neck …

I was so aroused by my husband at this moment. It was the first time since we had been married that we were having sex somewhere other than our bed. I put my hand through his arms and reached around to his back, feeling the muscles in his back contracting as he thrust in and out of me. I put my fingers on his shoulders to chase the tattoo lines, and I suddenly realised he didn't have any tattoos! I panicked... The feeling shocked me, and my heart instantly sank. *Kevin!* I cried out in my head. For the first time, I felt guilty! I actually felt ashamed for enjoying sex with my husband. Not only that, but I felt bad that I had agreed to stop taking my contraception medication in order to stop his constant nagging at me.

I kept trying to focus and enjoy this moment—I had wanted it for so long with Robbie—but I just couldn't shake the feeling! I could tell he was getting close, so for the first time in my life, I did it. I faked my first orgasm. I leaned my head back and started to take long deep breaths, slowly getting louder and deliberately making my body tremble. I gave one final loud moan and placed my hand onto his cheek. I then leaned my head forward and rested it on his chest. I looked up, and he smiled and kissed my forehead. "How was that!" he asked with a proud look on his face.

A moment later I felt him slowly thrust, then he thrusted hard and fast. I felt his body slightly shake as he kissed me and told me that that that was amazing. Then he thanked me for rethinking my decision on starting a family.

I gently reminded him, "There is no pressure, and it will happen when it happens—no trying. I'm still scared and not ready for this, Robbie. One day at a time, please!" I stressed to him. He agreed and took himself out of me, pulling up his pants. I slid myself off the bench and started cleaning up from dinner.

It wasn't long before Robbie was trying to keep track of my ovulation cycle. He was such a man's man, which made it so strange for me to deal with, and it just wasn't like him! I kept reminding him that we were supposed to be taking our time and we were going to let it happen when it happened. He began to hound me constantly for sex, and we were arguing all the time because his obsession with wanting a baby had become out of control. It was really stressing me out, but I had done it to myself by agreeing to take it slow and see what happened. I knew that if it felt right, I would feel different! I started wondering if it was because I didn't want to have his baby or if it really was me.

CHAPTER 9

The Right Timing

I HAD ALWAYS felt as if I were two people, but feeling and becoming are two very different things. I had become two completely different people in the past few months. One part of me was the boring housewife I had been for the past five years, and the other was this exhilarating and sexy free woman who was a mistress to her boss. I found my situation hard, for one woman was the life I thought I had always wanted and the other was the life I had always tried to avoid. I always knew I had that side of me, but I had always tried to control it. Robbie became so hard for me to cope with that I started having to cook valerian root and add it to his nightly tea just to get some peace from the baby talk.

Kevin and I spent a lot of time together; the more time we spent together, the more we found out about one another. He would tell me how lonely and unhappy he had been and for so long, saying that he would have divorced Kim a long time ago, but he didn't want to pay her out, as it was his family's money! He has slaved himself to the company since he was seventeen years old, just to prove himself to his father that he was ready to take over the company. She had never contributed, and he felt that she didn't deserve a cent. Therefore, they continued to live in separate wings of the house. He told me that at times he might not even see her for a week, and if he did, she usually wanted something from him, like money or for him to pay an account at a salon.

He'd known Kim from a young age and said she had always been so cold and selfish. He never wanted to marry her, and she was aware of that; his unhappiness in their marriage caused her hatred for him. He said that they tried to make it work for the first few years, but there just wasn't any life to her. He just couldn't mesh with her, and in the end, he couldn't even get it up for her. He said it was like having sex with a frozen skeleton! She was so lean and had no shape whatsoever; she was just so flat everywhere.

She wanted the relationship to work more than he did, as he believed she had always had a crush on him. They made an arrangement that they would stay together but they would basically live separate lives. He told me that this arrangement had worked for them both for around ten years and he would constantly sleep with other women. He said he had lost count of the amount of women he had slept with over the years, but he was always discreet, as he didn't want to rub these women in her face and upset her. They were always young model-looking women that he could pick up easily at the bar. He said he would park his car out the front of the bar or club, and the woman would just come to him. He told me that although he had had many lovers, there was always something missing in his life. He had control over the company, which was what he thought he had always wanted, and he had the house, car, and any women he wanted at the drop of a hat. But it was all just materialistic stuff, and those women made him feel even lonelier than he felt before.

I asked him, "Have you ever been in love?"

He replied, "There has not been one woman that I have ever met, or been with in the past, that I have thought about as I closed my eyes to go to sleep at night, so … the answer is no!" He smiled, but I could tell he was lying.

"Kevin, answer me this …"

"Depends," he responded.

"When was the last time you went to a bar and picked up a young model?"

He smiled as he realised I was on to him. "Honestly?" he asked.

"Yes, seriously! When was the last time you hooked up with a young model?" I asked him inquisitively.

"Around ten months ago." Having regrettably answered my question, he then quickly deferred the conversation and asked me about Robbie—how we met, what happened to my marriage, and whether Robbie made me happy.

I always tried to keep it vague with Kevin. But for some reason, for the first time in my life, I felt I could talk to someone else and that the person understood. I felt that Kevin was so similar to me; we both shared similar fears and pain. I explained to him that I didn't know if I ever really loved Robbie. I thought I did, but the last few months, I felt different about him and wasn't sure if I ever did. I told him, "My marriage makes me feel as if I'm dead on the inside, cold and alone … Every day is the same, Groundhog Day! I know that's life, but I'm bored. I'm just not sure if it's the life I want for myself for the next fifty years!" I took a pause, then a deep breath, and said, "You know what, Kevin? I have never cheated on anyone in the past. You are the first man other than Robbie I have been with in the past seven years!"

He apologised to me and then went on to tell me he couldn't help it. He told me he was drawn to me and was sorry he had put me in this position.

I told him he didn't have to apologise; we were both adults, and we had made these decisions together. I could tell he was interested in every word I was saying, almost as if he was captivated by me. I didn't know why, because while I was saying all of this, I was wearing my emotionless look on my face as Kevin sat in the seated position of the couch and I continued to lay my body over his, resting my head on the raised side of the couch. I told him that Robbie had been pressuring me for a baby.

I had never seen Kevin move as quickly as he did. He twisted his neck and head around in my direction with a stunned look on his face. My comment certainly got his attention! He asked me as he slightly sat up straight and fidgeted with his fingers on top of my stomach. "Well, what do you think about that? Do you want to have his baby, Ella?" he asked as his anxiety started to increase. I didn't say a word. I just continued to look into his eyes. He started to play nervously with the buttons on my shirt and then said, "I've always wanted a family. I don't think I've ever told you that!" He ran his fingers up and down my blouse, trailing his fingers from my breasts to my stomach. He laughed and said, "You're keeping me in suspense, girl."

I replied, "I think that Robbie only wants me to have a baby because he feels that I'm slipping away from his grip and it's the only way he can continue to control me!" Kevin nodded in agreement. This conversation surprised me, as we had never discussed the baby subject before, but I could see a little sparkle in Kevin's eyes as his fingers ran up and down my blouse. Then I watched his eyes suddenly turn jealous as he realised my baby would be with Robbie and not him. He continued to play with my buttons on my blouse and started to ask me more questions about my past.

"Tell me more, tell me more!" he said in a cheeky voice. He wanted to know about my parents. He had remembered that I had mentioned my mother at the Pink Owl Ball and asked me if I had any siblings.

I told him, "My father committed suicide when I was ten years old, my mother passed away two years ago from a brain tumour, and I have one brother named Luke. He's married, has three children, and lives in Queensland." I explained that I saw my brother once a year at Christmastime, Boxing Day. After we had spent Christmas Day with Robbie's family, we always flew up there and spent a week with my brother and my niece and nephews. He then asked me about my father's suicide—what happened and how he did it.

I explained to him as I continued lie on the couch, with him playing with my hair, lightly twisting it. "My mother's father became really ill. My grandfather was a beautiful man—warm, happy, a life-loving man—and he loved me unconditionally. I adored him! He had prostate cancer and didn't have long to live. My mother got the phone call one night saying that his health had dramatically declined. She spoke to my father, and he agreed that she could stay with her parents until her father passed. As we only had one vehicle, my father said that on the weekend, we would drive up as a family and drop her off, and he would look after us for a week or so. It was a four-hour drive north into no man's land.

"We got to my grandparents' house and spent the afternoon with them. We had lunch, and my brother and I said our goodbyes to our grandfather. Then my father said we had better be on our way, as it was a long and dangerous drive at night. We spent the next two weeks with my father looking after us. I remember late on the Friday night when the phone rang. My father answered the phone and said it was my mother, telling us that my grandfather had finally passed away. He told us his funeral was on the following Monday and that we wouldn't be going to school, that we would be going to the funeral and then bringing our mother home afterwards.

"My grandfather's funeral was the saddest day of my life, and I had never loved anyone in my life like I did that man! After the service, we went to the pub for a couple hours for the wake. My father drank a lot, as usual, but he didn't normally drink that much in public. He started to get loud and pushy towards people, and my mother suggested that we make our way home. He agreed, and my mother started to drive us all back home.

"Just over halfway home, my mother and brother were hungry. She asked my father if he would mind if she pulled over at the next lookout, as she had grabbed some food from the wake and it was in the boot of the car. She had brought enough to make a couple of sandwiches to get us by. We stopped at the next lookout, as my mother had requested, and the lookout was at the top of a cliff right on the edge of the ocean. My brother stayed with my mother to help her prepare lunch ... and pinch the food as she made it!" I laughed.

"I walked over to the edge and was mesmerized by the majestic view as I watched the waves crash onto the rocks below us. My father staggered over to where I was standing and stood right next to me. We just stood there side by side for a few minutes, in awe of the view, as it was truly spectacular. 'Ella,' he said, 'I just want to say I am sorry for what I am about to do ... I love you so much; you will always be my little angel!' He said this in his drunken stumbling state. He then put his hand on my hand and squeezed it tightly. He gave me a kiss on the forehead and then let go of my hand. All of a sudden, he started running for the cliff and just jumped! I tried to grab his hand, but it was too late …" As I said those last words, Kevin took a deep long-drawn-out breath and put his hands over his mouth in shock.

I continued. "I screamed and watched his weightless body fall slowly through the air, almost as if my life had turned into slow motion! I urgently started to scream out to my mother and point to the cliff's edge, screaming, 'He jumped, Mum! Help—he jumped!' My mother had already started to run towards me from my first squeal. She looked over the edge and put her hands to mouth, looking utterly devastated. She fell to her knees and began to cry hysterically. I hugged her and tried to relax her as she held on to my legs. Her cries got louder. My brother ran over and fell to my mother; he put his arms around her and started to cry as well. As I held my brother and mother, an old ute pulled up only minutes later and asked us if we were okay. Continuing to comfort my mother, I told the man our father had just jumped off the cliff and he was dead! He looked shocked and told me he would go into town and send us help.

"Within twenty minutes, a police car arrived. Two gentlemen got out of the car. One approached my mother and said, 'I am so sorry, ma'am, for your loss.' He put a blanket around her and asked her if he could take us back into town. The officer could tell my mother had gone into shock. As she sobbed, she nodded. The officer gently walked us over to the car.

"When we got to the station, the officer asked me a few questions, as I was the only one who witnessed what had happened. I told both of the male officers, 'He looked at me, said he was sorry, and jumped!' Both the officers looked at each other, stunned, and then looked back to me.

"The officer took my hand and said, 'I am sorry you had to witness that. I can't imagine how you are feeling right now. No one should ever have to go through what you are going through right now. If you ever need anything, please don't hesitate to come down the station or call me. I will always be here for you!'"

Kevin told me he couldn't believe that a man could do that to his own child—and how horrible it must have been for my family and me. He told me that the more he found out about me, the more I made sense to him, "the mystery behind the lipstick," as he liked to say.

He asked me about my mother's death, and I told him that my mother was a great woman. She had been a victim to my father's abuse until the day he died. She then became a single mother. She had never worked previously and had to start her life all over again. She worked so hard to keep a roof over our heads and keep us all safe. As free as she was from my father's torment, she still felt so much pain for his death! She would make comments every now and then, saying, "I thought your father was too selfish to do that! Why did he did it?" I believe she took his death personally, and she felt that he had left and abandoned her.

Five years later, she bumped into the police officer from my father's suicide. He asked her out on a date, and they ended up falling in love. He was a good man to her. I hadn't really seen him much, to be honest, since her death. I remember that when I was in my teens, she suffered with excruciating migraines. They got so bad sometimes that she would sometimes ask me to kill her. She didn't mean it; she just wanted the pain to stop. I believed all the head injuries she endured from my father's abuse had caused her migraines and then, later on, her brain tumour! I believed he was still tormenting her from his grave.

Kevin laughed awkwardly at me, and said, "I'm happy that she managed to find love in the end. It's nice listening to you talk. You are always so reserved, and you keep all this stuff to yourself … so it's nice to hear you talk about this stuff, Ella!"

I apologised to him and laughed for my past being so gloomy. Kevin put his arm around my neck and rested his hand on my chest. I snuggled my head into his neck. He kissed my forehead and then leaned his chin on my forehead. We simply sat there together as one.

CHAPTER 10

The New Client

AS WE ATE breakfast and organised our daily schedule the next day, Kevin told me we had a new client that he wanted to see after lunch. He wanted me to allow three hours in his schedule for the meet. That was a long time. I had been working by his side for the past eleven months, and he never had spent this much time with someone. I reconfirmed with him that he was sure he wanted me to allocate that amount time to one client. He told me that it was a long-time family friend. They had a lot of paperwork to complete, and vast decisions needed to be made. It was a beautiful sunny day, so I suggested to Kevin that considering we were going to be locked in a box for the three hours, possibly we could have lunch and go for a walk along the beach before the meeting. He thought that was a great idea.

We finished off all the paperwork and meetings for the morning and headed out for lunch. We went to our usual cafe for lunch. We sat on the lawn and ate before making our way down to the beach for a stroll. We took off our shoes and started to walk down the beach barefoot on the sand. Kevin was such a romantic at heart, so he loved moments like these. To be honest, I had never really been the romantic type, but I couldn't help but find it sweet when he took my hand. We had been walking for a good forty minutes when I realised the time and told Kevin we had to get back quickly! He wasn't concerned and said the client wouldn't be that stressed if we were ten minutes late.

We headed back over to the car park and rinsed the sand off our feet, using the towel from Kevin's boot to dry our feet before putting our shoes back on. We hopped back into the car and started heading in the direction of our next meeting. As we got closer, Kevin started acting strange. He said, "I'm so grateful for all the hours and energy you have given me—and the company—the past eleven months, Ella. We really appreciate all your hard work, and we don't take you for granted. Honestly, I wouldn't know what to do without you anymore. You are such an important asset to the company, and I just want you to know this."

I laughed. "All right, Kevin, you're getting a bit soft on me now!"

He laughed as well. "Well, as I was saying, we do really appreciate you, so the company has decided to give you something as a reward for all your hard work." I looked at him, confused as to what he was rambling on about … and then we pulled into a car dealership. At this point, I remembered that his family friend owned a Jaguar dealership—not a big surprise, as he has many wealthy contacts. He looked over and smiled at me. "So are you ready to pick and design your new car!"

"*What!* Are you serious?" I replied, shouting in shock. He nodded at me with a cheesy proud smile. "I can't, Kevin! It's too much … I really can't."

He looked at me so disappointedly, like a child who has just had his lunch stolen. "Please, Ella, I really want you to have a nice car! It's important to me. I want you to have it."

It didn't take me long to give in to him and his big beautiful brown puppy dog eyes. I looked over at him, opened my side door, and said, "Quickly, before I change my mind!"

As I got out of the car, I saw him smile and then wink at his mobile phone before putting in his pocket and getting out of his car. I thought that was strange behaviour for Kevin. As we closed the doors of Kevin's car, a gentleman was already approaching Kevin. Kevin gave him a handshake that turned into a man hug, slapping one another's backs. They were clearly happy to see one another and expressed how long it had been in-between drinks.

I walked around the car to Kevin's side, and he introduced me to Michael, his long-time friend from school. He told me that Michael owned the dealership and had come in today to help us out. Michael asked me if I knew the types of cars he had. I nodded, and they both seemed surprised.

I told them both, "I love the F-PACE, as it's the only SUV on the market with real grunt, and I love the front grill as its bold looking." They both looked at each other in surprise.

"Wow, Ella! That really surprises me. We can certainly look at the F-PACE for you!" said Kevin, a shocked look still on his face.

"I do have the top of the range in the showroom. I'll ask one of my staff members to move it out so you can take it for a test drive and see if you like it," Michael said to me. He headed over to a staff member.

I wrapped my arms around Kevin's neck and locked my fingers. I kissed him on his lips and just stayed in that position, telling him how surprised I was and that he really was a romantic, not to mention always full of surprises.

He was holding my lower back and rocking me in his arms. "I thought you'd like this," he said, seeming very pleased with himself.

"I really do!"

"Well, you have the next three hours to pick out colours for the exterior and interior, the type of sunroof you want, and decide whether you want glitter in your paint. You can have anything you want."

I told Kevin that I knew how lucky I was to have him in my life. Michael brought the car out for me to drive. I got into the driver's seat, and Kevin jumped into the passenger seat. Michael came over and started showing me all the features and how to use all the gadgets. I loved this car instantly. It was so ridiculously comfortable and had so much spunk! We took it for a drive, and I swear you couldn't have wiped the grin off my face if you tried. I felt so spoilt.

As I drove around for a good twenty minutes, Kevin had his hand in my lap the whole time, softy massaging my inner thigh. He was asking me all sorts of questions and wanting me to do different things to test the handling of the car. Typical male. But I didn't care. It was fast, luxurious, and had a hatch. I was in love! When we got back, Michael came out and asked us to come inside and have coffee and discuss the car. We went inside and sat down, and Kevin told Michael, "She hated it, absolutely hated it!" He burst into laughter.

Michael looked at me. "What did you think, Ella?"

"I loved it, Michael!" I replied, feeling so grateful.

They both seemed happy with my decision. Michael told me that now that I was happy with the car, I had to go through the selection process and build the car with the options I would like. I couldn't believe the options I had! I really was a small-town girl who had always driven small cheap hatchbacks. I had never cared for things like this, but I also had never previously had the opportunity either! I travelled in Kevin's car every day, and that was amazing. I must admit that after hours in his car and then returning to the office and getting into my Toyota

Yaris, it was more than slightly disappointing. Trust me! So I went through all the options with Michael, from picking the sunroof to the glitter white paint, rims, and then the colour of the interior. Michael told me I would have to wait a couple of weeks for the car to be ready, and he would contact Kevin as soon as it arrived.

Two weeks later, Kevin and I were in the office messing around with paperwork, getting ready for our next meeting, when Kevin's phone rang. He answered it. He seemed happy with the conversation, and when he hung up, he said, "Guess what, Ella."

"What?" I responded as I smiled at him, knowing that he was up to something.

"Your car's ready to pick up today!" he said as he waved his phone around in celebration.

I literally leaped out of my seat and ran over and jumped on him, wrapping my legs around his waist, screaming with enthusiasm. I was so excited about my new car. I kissed him repeatedly on his cheek, thanking him. As my legs were wrapped around Kevin's waist, I could feel Kevin start getting excited for other reasons. I told him no. He looked up at me, rather shocked as he continued to hold me. "Why?" he asked, seeming confused, as I had never refused him in the past.

I laughed and said, "Can we in my new car?"

He smiled and shook his head at me "You're so naughty! As if I am going to say no to that," he replied sarcastically. "Well, in that case, we'll catch a taxi to the meeting, and afterwards we will pick up your car, and then we can …" He mischievously rubbed his body against mine and then put his hands up my dress and grabbed hold of my arse cheeks. He squeezed them tightly and said, "Yes, that sounds more than great!"

We went to the meeting, and afterwards we were dropped off by the taxi to pick up my new car. I drove us back to the office, and as soon as I had parked the car and turned it off, I looked over at him and smiled. I then put my hands up my dress and slid my lace thong down my legs, throwing it at him, and then I wiggled my dress up to my waist and pulled it over my shoulders and my head. I unclipped my bra and threw that at him as well. I leaned over and kissed him on his lips. I then slowly pulled my head away from his and giggled at him, winking my right eye at him as I climbed naked into the back seat.

He bit his bottom lip and undid his belt, sliding off his pants and undoing his shirt. He then crawled into the back seat with me. As he climbed on top of me, he kept telling me how naughty I was and how much he loved it. We had sex, and it was so much fun. I giggled practically the entire time as he played around, nibbling at me, holding me down, and tickling me. I told him it was a must to have sex in my new car and thanked him for my gift. He kissed me and told me, "I adore you, Ella!" He then leaned down towards me and slowly kissed my forehead. "I wanted you to be in a vehicle that was safe and luxurious for my sexy girl."

As happy as I felt, I was dreading my future, as I knew that as soon as I drove this sexy, luxurious sports car into my driveway, it would cause a major fight with Robbie. As he was lying on top of me, still inside me, I told Kevin I was worried about Robbie's reaction to the car.

Kevin told me that if Robbie felt it was from the company, and not from Kevin, he might not react so badly. "To be honest, Ella, I wish that Robbie didn't exist at all! But he does, so I filmed us in the car that day when we first drove into the dealership, while I was talking about the business being grateful for all your hard work."

"So that's why you were acting strange that day and you winked at your phone?" I said, and he burst out laughing.

"You saw me do that!"

"Yes," I responded, joking around and calling him a dork. "So you did that so Robbie wouldn't get mad at your buying me luxurious gifts?"

"Yes, Ella. I couldn't have you driving around a Toyota Yaris! I've already tagged you on Facebook, thanking you and saying it was a gift from the company."

"Oh, *shit!*" I said aloud. All I could think of was Robbie having time to sit and stew about this. Then I thought, *I deserve this. I don't give a shit anymore. I love this car, and I will deal with whatever happens. Every action has a reaction, and I will deal with my reaction!*

As I drove home, I couldn't help but think that for a forty-three-year old man, he was excessively savvy with all the social media. He was trying to help me, but I couldn't help but think it was weird, and I'm not sure it would have helped my situation.

I got home, and Robbie was waiting in the driveway as I drove my new car in and parked. As I got out of the car and took my handbag from the passenger seat, Robbie came over to the car, greeted me with a kiss, and then closed the car door for me. "Nice new rig, Ella!" he said, acting inquisitive as he peeked inside.

"Please don't be mad, Robbie. Work gave it to me as a gift for working hard. There's nothing else to it," I stressed to him. His response shocked me.

"Well ... okay then. If you're happy, I'm happy!" He took my handbag and carried it inside the house for me, placing it down on the kitchen counter. That was it! No fighting, no questions, nothing. I felt that was strange, and it had me more concerned.

Kevin messaged me, as I knew he would be worried about Robbie's reaction as well. I told him Robbie was cool with it and happy for me. He immediately sent me back a shocked emoji. I was as taken back by Robbie's reaction as much as Kevin was.

I was trying to work out what was going on, why Robbie was being so nice to me. My thoughts were flooding my mind, and I was trying to sift and sort through them. As I was doing so, I remembered a statement Kevin had made earlier today that had shocked me and had no relevance to what I was trying to work out. It was when Kevin had said that he wished Robbie didn't exist. I did understand that it would be hard for him to watch me go home to another man every night, but I was surprised he said it aloud.

I went over to the kettle and pushed down the lever to boil the water. Robbie came over to me and put his hand on my lower back, saying, "I was hoping we could watch a movie or something tonight, as I know you'll be out tomorrow night."

I told him that sounded nice, and that's when I finally realised why Robbie was acting strangely. It was my birthday tomorrow, but today was the first day of my monthly ovulation, and Robbie wanted to try for a baby!

CHAPTER 11

$\mathcal{M}$y Birthday

TODAY WAS MY birthday, and I was thirty-two years old. People have always told me that after thirty, it's all downhill from there, but I tend to disagree. My age didn't frighten me. It was more about the person I was rather than the number of my age. My birthday wasn't something I told people about. I don't like a lot of fuss, and I don't like to have parties, so I don't see the point. However, I do have a tradition with my two best friends: every year for our birthdays, we pick a venue and have a girls' night out on the town. As we truly only catch up a few times a year due to work and family commitments, the times we do catch up, it's an event, so our husbands are also with us. Our girls' nights are about the only times a year where we can truly tell each other what's going and just be ourselves.

The nights normally end up with my head face down in the toilet and me telling myself, "I will never drink again!" Of course, Robbie gives me no sympathy whatsoever, saying, "It was all self-inflicted!" But I do look forward to these nights, even though I know how they will end. I get to pick where I would like to go, then dress up, look glamorous, and dance, as I hardly ever go out as it is; plus, my husband isn't there. It has become something special to us. We never do gifts. It's just show up and drink, and then dance, and then more drinking until one of us calls it a night. Normally that happens when one of us can no longer dance due to the severe pain and cramps in our feet or the room is spinning and one of us can no longer stand—always classy nights!

As it was my birthday, the girls had sent me a text message a couple of days ago, wanting to know where we were meeting for drinks. I told them to meet me at CC and Co Tavern, a local bar, at seven. I've been there a few times in the past, and it has always had a great atmosphere. As it was a Friday, it was the busiest night of the week. It was only about twenty minutes from my work and around thirty minutes from home. It was good location for the girls as well.

I woke up and got Robbie ready for work. He kissed me goodbye and wished me a happy birthday, saying he hoped I had a great girls' night out. Before he left, he stopped at the door, turned around, and told me that he had just one request for the evening. I asked him what it was, and he asked me to just text him every so often, just to check in and let him know that everything was okay. I agreed, kissed him goodbye, and got ready for work.

At work, I spent the day with Kevin as usual, in and out of meetings all morning. Over lunch, he asked me what my plans were for the weekend. I told him that I was meeting up with my friends that night after work for some drinks. He asked me if it was for a particular occasion, and I told him that a couple of nights a year, we all catch up and just eat, drink, and dance, adding that we had been doing this since we were twenty years old, well before any of us were married.

I asked him what his plans were, and he told me he had his cousin's Bachelor party. I wished him the best of luck, telling him that if he didn't show on Monday, I'd know why. He laughed and told me he hated those kinds of nights. He told me he used to find them humorous and fun, but as he got older, he found them to be loud and sleazy. He told me he had witnessed, and tried to stop, his mates from doing so many stupid things that they ended up regretting, things that changed their lives forever.

After we had finished work for the day, I kissed him goodbye and wished him a great weekend. Kevin was also leaving straight away to head over to his cousin's bachelor party. I'd let him know that I was leaving my car in the car park and getting a taxi there and home, as I was a bit paranoid about my new car. At least I knew that our car park and building had security to get in and out, so I felt it would be reasonably safe there. I could tell he wasn't happy about the taxi, so I told him that I would get a taxi to the bar and then organise for one of the husbands to pick us up. He told me he was happier about that plan and hoped that I had a lovely night out with the girls. I went off to the bathroom and did my make-up, put some loose curls through my hair, applied my fake lashes, and slid on my dress and heels.

Even though it was February, late summer weather in Melbourne is unpredictable. All year is actually unpredictable; it's all over the place. The nights could be randomly fresh and tonight was going to be a cold one, so I threw on my jacket and went down the lifts, waiting for the taxi out front. When it arrived, I jumped in and he drove me to my destination.

I walked into the bar with my little black dress, nude four-inch heels, and my white fake fur coat. As I looked around the room, I noticed that the others were already there siting in the booth seating waiting for me. I walked over to them at the table, took my coat off, and threw it on the far side, were the booth met the wall. I gave them both a cuddle and a kiss on their cheeks. As they were squizzing me at the same time, they were both cuddling me and yelling into my ear, "Happy birthday, Ella!" in singsong voices and kissing my cheeks.

I sat down at the four-person booth. Kristina was sitting to my left. She was the funniest, craziest girl I have ever known, loud and overly opinionated—that is most likely an understatement for her. She was as bold as a bull and wore her heart on her sleeve. She was always honest, and she would always tell you how she saw it, even if you didn't want to hear it!

Then there was Sophie, who was so beautiful and kind in so many ways. She was the only one of us girls who had a pure judgement-free heart. I was not as bad as Kristina, but was not kind like Sophie either. We all seemed to have different quirks about us, but the three of us kept each other evenly balanced. We could only see each other a few times a year, as I said, but every time we got together, it felt as if no time had passed in between drinks. They had always been my sisters, my chosen family.

Kristina was looking sexy per usual, wearing a strappy nude bodysuit with a black leather miniskirt, and Sophie was always looking gorgeous but far more conservative, wearing an above-knee white lace dress. Kristina oozed confidence and sex appeal. She was just fabulous in every way, whereas Sophie was the girl next door. We called her the nun. It's so funny how different we all were.

As soon as I sat down, Kristina started yelling out to the waitstaff. "We need a dirty martini for the birthday girl and a round of Kahlúa hazelnut shots for the table, please!" The girl at the bar gave us the thumbs up, and a couple of minutes later, our drinks arrived. Kristina started to speak, her voice increasing in volume. "What's different with you, babe? You seem different!" I laughed but told her nothing. "Ella, you have this powerful sexiness to you, like you ... like you finally don't care what people think of you. I love it! It's sexy as all hell, babe. That dark cloud that used to hover is finally gone. Whoever you're fucking, keep doing it—it's working!" I just sat there in shock but then couldn't help burst out laughing. It was so typical Kristina—that's just who she was.

Sophie nudged Kristina. "You can't say that, Kristina. What about Robbie!"

Kristina winked at me and continued to laugh aloud. We each grabbed a shot each and raised it towards the ceiling, up to head height. Kristina always made the toasts, so Sophie and I always waited to see what Kristina would come up with this time.

"Cheers to whoever Ella is fucking!" "Cheers to whoever I am fucking!" I said as I drank down my first shot, and then I burst out in laughter again.

"Aw, and … happy birthday!" said Kristina.

I started to sip my dirty martini, which has always been favourite alcoholic beverage, and Kristina was already ordering another two rounds of shots. I smiled at Sophie and winked at her, as at this point, we both realised we were in for a wild night. Sophie thought it would be a great idea to get some food. We ordered some antipasto platters for the table for us to nibble on, to try to suppress the alcohol as much as possible. The conversation and drinks flowed, along with lots of laughter, as the three of us always had lots of catching up to do.

Kristina asked me, "How is your perfect Robbie going these days?"

Long story … Robbie cannot stand Kristina, as he cannot cope with how loud and abrupt she can be, so they have clashed many times in the past. Kristina has always been like my bossy big sister, so she is very protective over me, and she hates Robbie with a passion.

I laughed and told her in a sarcastic tone, "My perfect Robbie is doing fine!" I took another sip of my drink and asked her how her husband, Phil, was going. She told me he was good. He was at home with their two children. She said she had prepared homemade pizzas for them for dinner, and they were watching football together. She told me how she was always concerned that having a child meant that her husband would leave all the chores up to her, but since their first child, he had really stepped up, and even more so since their second child, saying that they were just so happy together. I felt so happy for Kristina. She had always been such an amazing person and friend, and I honestly felt so much joy for her. She truly deserved it.

Sophie's partner, Jake, proposed to her six months ago, so she was in full crazy bride-to-be mode, trying to plan everything and stressing out about every little of detail to make the day perfect. We just laughed and told her that on the day, none of that stuff matters. You forget and just enjoy the day. People don't notice all the things you have ripped your hair out for months planning. As long as there is booze, music, food, a bride and groom, and somewhere for people to dance, they really don't care or remember the rest. As Kristina and I had both been there, we found it funny and were both so relieved that we had been there and done that!

Sophie's phone rang, and she flashed it to show us it was Jake, telling us she was just going to pop outside for a few minutes. He'd just be checking in to see how she was going. We laughed and teased her about how cute he was.

As soon as Sophie left the room, Kristina said, "You seem so happy, Ella. I am so happy to see you like this. Again, you have this sexy, confident look—and I think the most cleavage I have ever seen you with! You have always been so beautiful, but you have always had a sadness about you."

I laughed and told her, "I do feel very different within myself! I feel like something has sparked inside me, that I am finally alive."

"I love you so much! It is so great to see you like this, honey. So here comes my next question: when are you asking Robert for a divorce?" She giggled.

I picked up my martini and started to scull it down. Kristina looked around the room, waving her hand up in the air. She got the attention of a gentleman working at the bar and yelled out for another two rounds of shots and another drink each. She looked back at me, shaking her head. "Why is it we have been friends for so long and I still need to pry any information out of you, Ella? I will get you smashed, and you will tell me everything!" she told me as she passed me a shot. I slammed down the shot, and she passed me another one immediately. We clinked our shots together and slammed them down. I started tapping my hands on the edge of the table, as the rush from the alcohol was going straight to my head.

Kristina said, "You forget that I was your matron of honour at your wedding, and I did try to tell you that just because you are a woman doesn't mean you have to have a normal life and get married and have babies like everyone else. I love my life! I love being a wife and a mother; you know that. But you have always been different. That's what makes you so beautiful. My happy life isn't your ideal happy life, and there's nothing wrong with that! So when are you asking him for a divorce?"

I took a deep breath. "It's not that simple, Kristina. I don't know if I can!" I replied as I took the last sip from my drink. "He wants a baby." I held my glass in the air, getting the last drops of alcohol out of the glass, as Sophie returned to the table all cute and giggly from talking to her husband-to-be on the phone.

Kristina was staring at me with a stunned look upon her face. "I hope you're not going to give him what he wants. Ella?" Kristina questioned me, seeming concerned.

Sophie sat down and said, "I noticed before, and thought I was seeing things, but as I have gone and come back and it's still the same, I'm going to say something. You know me—I don't normally say this—but have you girls noticed the incredibly handsome man at the far table staring over here!"

Kristina said, "Yeah, he's really hot … I do know the face from somewhere. I just can't work out who he is or where I have seen him!"

I was so curious, and I asked the girls where this guy was sitting so I could peek a look at him. Sophie pointed to my far right behind me. I slowly turned my head around to have a look, and as soon as I saw him, I quickly turned my head straight back around and laughed.

Kristina saw the look on my face and automatically started pointing towards me. "Aww … Ella, I know who it is. It's just come to me." she laughed. "It's your boss!" I nodded to let her know she had guessed correctly. "I remember his face from that ball you went to. The pics were on Facebook … and that video that was posted about your new car!"

I looked back at Kevin, smiled, and waved to him. He was sitting at a table with around thirty drunken blaring guys! He got up and came over to our table. He placed one hand on my shoulder, standing to my right, and the first thing he said was, "Happy birthday, Ella!" with a surprised look on his face. He then reached his hand over to Kristina and introduced himself. "Hi, I'm Kevin, Ella's boss."

Kristina replied as she shook his hand, "Kristina."

"Nice to meet you, Kristina!" said Kevin.

"Nice to meet you too, Kevin. I have heard so much about you!" She had a cheeky, flirtatious look on her face.

He moved his hand over to Sophie, and she told him her name.

"Nice to meet you both! But that would surprise me, Kristina. Trying to get any information out of this one is like pulling teeth," he replied as he looked down at me with a sarcastic smile.

Kristina laughed and told him, "The trick is that you have to get her pissed—that's what I do—and then you get little bits and pieces. It's like a puzzle, but you still have to work the rest out yourself!"

He also laughed and agreed with her. Kevin's table started to yell out to him to come back. "Kevo, hurry up, man. Chase tail later. Shots, man!" He looked back, laughed, and wished us all a great night before returning to his table.

As soon as he walked away, Kristina started with me. "OMG, he is hotter in real life! How do you work with that man every day?"

Sophie nudged Kristina. "He is hot—even I will admit that—but Ella has Robbie. And didn't you see that Kevin's married? Kristina!"

"How's the new car going, Ella? Is that the only reward you get for working with him?" asked Kristina, laughing hysterically and throwing her head back.

I replied, "The new car is amazing. I love it! Okay, girls, I will admit that I have a really good job." I clamped my hands together.

"Finally!" yelled Kristina.

Sophie shook her head with disapproval at Kristina and me. She got up from the table and let us know she needed to go to the bathroom. Kristina realised she needed to go to the bathroom as well, and she got up with Sophie. I then told the girls I'd order another round of drinks while they were gone. I got up and went over to the bar.

As I was leaning against the bar waiting to be helped, two men came up to me and leaned on the bar on either side of me. The men were standing so close that they were almost literally touching me. They started asking my name and telling me how beautiful I was, the normal guy thing, trying every trick in the book, with their pathetic pickup lines, trying to get into my pants. I was pretty conditioned to this behaviour, and I started laughing because they were so drunk and lame that I couldn't help myself. I put my left hand up towards the ceiling and told them, "Sorry, boys. I'm married!" I waved my hand in the air, showing them my wedding ring.

The man on my right showed me his wedding ring and said, "Me too. No strings attached—even better!" I just laughed in shock and then shook my head at him. This guy was confident!

The bar staff asked me what I would like, and I told them another round of drinks and shots for our table—and to change my dirty martini to raspberry vodka. As I started to turn around to get away from the sleazy men next to me, I heard a familiar voice whisper in my ear, "That ring hasn't stopped you in the past!" As I continued to turn around, I saw Kevin standing directly behind me. He startled me.

The guys start to nudge each other, disappointed, and one said, "Kevo's here. We don't stand a chance now!" They rolled their eyes at one another.

I held a hand to my chest, as my heart was racing. "You scared me, Kevin!" I told him as I tried to catch my breath. Kevin was standing right in my face, staring expressionless at me.

"Bruce, Tom, this is Ella, my assistant," he said. "Ella, this is Bruce and Tom."

"That's your assistant? Wow, I thought I was jealous of you before!" Bruce said.

"Do you boys mind giving us a moment?" Kevin asked them. They nodded and walked back towards their table. Kevin leaned close to my body, holding his hands on the bar behind me. "I cannot believe you, Ella! I spent the day with you, and you never told me even once that it's your birthday today." Kevin said this to me with a disappointed, pissed off look on his face.

"What do you want me to say, Kevin? I'm not a birthday person!" I was still trapped by his muscular arms and chest at the bar.

"I am just so disappointed—I wish I had known! I could have done so many things for you!" he said to me as he lightly pinched and held my chin.

"That's why I didn't tell you; I knew you would spoil me. How is the bachelor party going? Your cousin looks like he's having fun!" I said to Kevin, trying my best to defer the conversation off me.

"It's been a good night so far! We're supposed to be going to the strippers next."

"That should be fun for you."

"Ella, you know I am only interested in seeing a certain women naked!" he said to me as he took his hand off my chin and started to twist the ends of my curled hair.

I took a deep breath and said, "We can't do this, Kevin—not here!"

He let go of my hair, taking a step back and completely moving away from me. I couldn't tell at this point if he had had too much to drink or if he was just upset with me. I put a hand on either side of his face and told him, "I am sorry … I should have told you. I just knew you would have done something special for me. And the truth is, I love your attention and your romantic gestures any other day, but on my birthday, Kevin, I am very different. I'm so sorry I have upset you!" I was trying to reassure him because I couldn't stand seeing him like this.

It broke my heart to look at him. I knew he felt that I'd lied to him. It wasn't about my birthday; it was the fact that I had deliberately kept it from him that really upset him.

The girls started to walk towards the table as the drinks arrived. I took my hands off his face and kissed him on his cheek. Heading back over to the table and standing at the edge, I picked up my shot and then my drink and sculled both down. I then slammed my glasses on the table and held my forehead until the alcohol pain passed. I told the girls it was time to dance. I could seriously feel the alcohol going to my head, and I had to get away from Kevin because at this point I was beyond tipsy. I was borderline drunk, and I was scared. As the man drew me in, he was soon becoming my Achilles heel. I knew I had to stay away from him; otherwise, our cover would be completely blown! He seemed okay as he walked back over to his table.

The three of us girls made our way over to the dance floor and started to dance in a protected closed triangle to avoid letting anyone in. We were all so drunk and having so much, jumping and being silly to the music. The dance floor was packed, so we could feel people all around us pushing, touching, and grabbing our bodies. I looked around the room, and we were fully surrounded by men dancing around us. Kristina couldn't stop laughing; she had always loved the attention. I looked over and saw Kevin standing just off the dance floor, facing his body in our direction watching us, as he was in conversation with one of the guys from the bachelor party. He reminded me of like a protective big brother—in this case, my protective lover.

We had been dancing and singing for a good forty minutes, and I was feeling hot and sweaty. I had the driest throat from screaming out the lyrics to the music, so I told the girls I was going to get a drink from the bar and asked them if they wanted one while I was there. I went up to the bar and asked the server for a water and a raspberry vodka. She gave me the water and then, a moment later, the vodka. I turned my body around, leaning my back against the bar, taking tiny sips from the water and watching my friends dancing. I loved seeing how much fun they were having. I looked over in the direction of where Kevin had been standing and couldn't see him there anymore. I felt someone slide up against me and pump my hip. I looked over, and it was Kevin.

"I think that's a great idea." He winked as I continued to sip the water slowly. "Do you know how sexy you look tonight? I wish I could take you home with me," he softly whispered in my ear. He began to run his fingers slowly up and down the front of my thigh as we stood side by side, both facing the dance floor.

I agreed with him and kissed him on the cheek. I grabbed the vodka. "Want to dance with us ... *Kevo?*" I started to giggle, teasing him. "Come on—I have to dance. I love dancing so much!" I took his hand and walked onto the dance floor towards my friends, still holding his hand and dragging him through the crowd.

He started dancing with us, and then Kevin caught the eyes of his mates. They all decided to come over, including the groom-to-be. We were all dancing together, jumping all around, each of us soaking wet from sweating and laughing. His mates kept telling me what a great bloke Kevin was. We had danced for a good two hours, going back and forth from the bar to the dance floor, when I started to feel a bit light-headed. My feet were killing me from jumping around in four-inch heels, and they were starting to go numb, which was worse because I didn't really have the strength or any feeling to lift my feet. I did it to myself every time, but I knew I had just reached my limit. I told the girls my feet were hurting and it might be time to go. They both agreed with me.

I also told Kevin I was ready to go home. He asked me how we were getting home, and I told him we were all catching the same taxi and getting dropped off to our homes. He asked if I wanted him to drop us home, and I told him he had had far too much to drink and we would be fine catching a taxi, adding that I would see him on Monday. I kissed him goodbye on his cheek and started to make my way back to the table. However, he took my arm and said, "You're not hopping in an taxi, Ella. I've told you that!"

I laughed and then cheekily flicked his tie, smiling at him as I continued to head back over to our table. After we'd gathered our stuff and walked through to the exit, we made our way out to the front of the bar. I pulled out my phone to order a taxi. Kevin walked over to Kristina and Sophie, asking them if they would like him to drive us all home. He told them he didn't trust cab drivers on the best of days, especially not with three beautiful drunk women, and he was worried about it. They were both so happy and told him he was so sweet, taking him up on his offer immediately. He walked up behind me looking rather pleased with himself and rubbed my shoulders quickly as if he were going to give me a massage. He told me he was going to get his car and would be right back.

It felt as if we were only waiting a minute when Kevin pulled up in his car. The girls were so excited, and Kristina was so thrilled that she let out a small squeal of excitement. "Look at his car! OMG, Ella!" she said as she held her hand over her mouth. She opened the door and slid her body into the back seat of his car. She was automatically loud and excited, telling Kevin he had the sexist car she had ever seen and adding that it was the sexist car she had ever been in. He asked the girls where they lived so he could work out whom he dropped off first. Sophie was always dropped off first, as she was the closest to the city, and I was always the last one, as I am a country bumpkin.

When we got to Sophie's house, Kevin pulled into her driveway. She thanked Kevin for dropping her home and wished me a happy birthday. She told Kristina and me, "I had such a wonderful evening tonight! Thank you, girls. I love you both so much! And before I forget, can you two get your act together and show up for your dress fittings, please? I'm getting married in three months' time and still don't have your dresses ordered!"

Kristina and I both started to groan and laugh. "Yes, yes, Sophie, we will get the dresses sorted"

"We will call you this week. Love you! Now get out," said Kristina.

Sophie blew us both kisses and closed the door. We started driving to Kristina's house, and Kristina didn't stop talking the entire way, telling Kevin her whole life story, about her marriage, her kids, her work, you name it. A fifteen-minute drive turned into an hour. I rested my head on the headrest and closed my eyes. I was so drunk that I could feel the space spinning in pulses repeatedly. I tried to drown out my best friend's voice ... I loved her, but my God, could she talk.

Before I knew it, I had completely fallen asleep. I woke up to Kristina slugging me goodbye and kissing me on the cheek. She wished me a happy birthday and told me how much she loved me. She got out of the car and walked over to Kevin's window. She gave him a kiss on the cheek and thanked him for looking after us tonight. Kristina then told him my address, as I probably would fall back asleep again, and then she whispered into Kevin's ear. I could only faintly hear her tell him, "Do not go inside. Drop Ella off at the end of her driveway and run. Don't let Robbie see you. Trust me!" She stepped away from the car, waved, and then put her hand into her purse to find her keys to unlock her front door.

Kevin reversed out of her driveway and headed in the direction of my house. He put his hand on my knee and asked me if I had had a good night. I told him, "Yes, I did. I love my catch-ups with those girls. They mean the world to me and always have. I don't have a lot of family, and I don't have any in Melbourne, so they are the only family I have here."

"I completely understand what you're saying. But, Ella, just because you have gone through many things in your life alone, it doesn't mean that you still have to! Honestly, I am here," he stressed to me as he massaged my thigh.

I told him with an urgent tone to my voice, "Kevin, pull over the car, please!" He pulled over immediately. I climbed over the gear stick and squeezed my lower back past the steering wheel. Climbing on top of him, keeping myself in a seated squatting position facing him, I put my hands on his face, running my fingers through his facial hair on his lower cheek. I tilted my head and slowly started to kiss him on his lips. I pulled my head away from his and looked into his eyes in my drunken state with my slurring voice. "I want to run away! I need to get away from this place, Kevin." I squeezed his face and kissed him again.

He asked me, "Do you want to stay at my house for the night? You can tell Robbie that you have stayed at Kristina's. He won't look for you there!"

I told him I shouldn't and climbed back and sat in my chair. I could tell right away that he felt he'd said done something wrong, but I was honestly too drunk to care! I could feel my eyes trying to force themselves to close. I was trying so hard to fight it. Moments later, I had completely passed out. I woke up, opened my eyes, and saw my ceiling fan. I suddenly realised I was lying on my bed in my house.

I could hear Robbie talking to Kevin. My heart began to race. *Oh my God!* Kevin was in my house … with my husband. My fears had come into the present, and I was honestly terrified! I could hear Kevin explaining that it was a coincidence that we both had events at the same venue.

He awkwardly laughed and said to Robbie, "You know your wife, Robbie. Even if I asked her where she was going out, she wouldn't have told me!"

Robbie laughed in agreeance and then told Kevin, "When I first met Ella, I had to find out when my birthday was off Sophie because she wouldn't tell me herself!"

Kevin seemed confused and curious. He asked Robbie, "Why is she so funny about her birthday?"

"I don't know if you know, but it's the same day her old man killed himself. They were all so preoccupied with her grandfather's funeral, that they all forgot it was Ella's birthday. Then her old man jumped that afternoon! I only found that out from one of the girls as well! That's why the girls take her out for her birthday. They've been doing it for around the past twelve years now, I think." He thanked Kevin for dropping me home and apologised to Kevin for almost punching him when he walked in the door.

I heard the front door shut and quickly pulled myself out of bed. My throat was dry and felt as if I had drank sand. I headed into the kitchen and poured myself a glass of water. As I was filling my glass with water from the tap, Robbie came into the kitchen. He saw me and immediately walked over to me and gave me a kiss on my lips. "How's the head? I just met your boss ... or should I say your *special friend*, Ella!" He said this with aggression in his tone of voice as I continued to take slow sips out of my glass of water. "You are his PA ... and you're not even in management. First he buys you a very expensive car and now he's dropping you home drunk on a Friday night! I'm trying to work all this out, Ella. I may be a country boy, but I'm not fucking stupid. I can tell he cares for you!"

I placed my empty glass down on the bench. As his anger levels were increasing towards me, I walked past him and made my way to the bedroom, not even giving a slight reaction to his comments. I moved my hair out of the way and reached to the back of my dress. I started to unzip it, pulling my arms out of the dress and then sliding it off my body until it fell to the floor. Robbie came up behind me and started kissing my neck. He slid his hands under my arms and squeezed my breasts from behind. I grabbed his hands and took them off my body. I turned around and faced him, and then I kissed him on the lips and told him, "Not tonight, Robbie! Goodnight. I am going to bed. I'm so tired, and my feet are so sore!" I went over to my side of the bed and fell straight asleep.

The next day, I woke up and immediately looked at my phone to check the time. I was shocked. I had slept until lunchtime. I never slept in. I had heaps of messages from Kevin and Kristina. I started scrolling through them, reading both of their messages. They both had pretty much been sending me the same messages; they were just checking I was okay. Kristina wanted to know Robbie's reaction to Kevin dropping me off, and Kevin wanted to know what happened after he left. I replied to Kristina's messages, telling her that I was fine and would catch up with her. We needed to organise a time for the dress fitting.

I got out of bed, and I felt so sick. I knew I had had way too much to drink last night. I walked around the house to see where Robbie was, as I felt I should probably call Kevin because I remembered parts of the night but not everything! I walked into the kitchen and looked out the window. I could see Robbie in the far paddock, hitting a fence post into the ground. I leaned my body against the bench and then pulled myself up using my arms. I then sat on top of the bench so I could keep an eye on Robbie the entire duration of my phone call. I felt it was safe, so I called Kevin. I felt a bit nervous about calling him. I knew I had hurt him by not telling him it was my birthday … and then I thought back about the car ride home!

He answered the phone straight away, as if he had been waiting all morning for my phone call. I told him I was fine and that I was sorry if I was a handful last night—that I didn't tell him it was my birthday and that it was a selfish thing of me to do! He told me not to apologise and that he completely understood why I am funny about the day. He apologised for being so pushy about it. He told me it was so nice to see me out with my friends. "You looked so beautiful and happy last night, Ella. I mean, you always look beautiful, but last night you were so sexy, fun, and free!

"Thank you! I felt like it. I had so much fun; I always do with those girls. They bring out the wild child in me, as do you … Thank you for bringing me home and dropping the girl's home as well. I don't even remember how I got into the house!"

He laughed and said, "Well, that was interesting! Kristina warned me when I dropped her off home last night that when I reached your house, I should drop you off at the end of the driveway and bail!" Kevin burst out in laughter. "I couldn't do that. I didn't even want to take you back there, but as it was the last thing you said before you passed out, I respected your wishes. So I bit the bullet and pulled up in your driveway. I took your seat belt off and tried to get you out of the car without hitting your head. I just about had you in my arms to carry you when I heard what sounded like your house door swing open. I heard fast footsteps coming towards me. That's when I heard your charming husband start shouting and ranting at me. I let you go, and he was asking and demanding me to tell him what I had done to you. I quickly turned around, and he started pushing me, grabbing my shirt and slamming me into my car—and then he was trying to choke me!"

"*Oh my God!* Are you serious? I am so sorry and embarrassed he did that to you!" I felt so ashamed.

"Yeah, he was pulling on my jacket, and I was yelling at him that you were just drunk and I only brought you home. He didn't believe me, and then I grabbed him firmly, shook him, and told him, 'If I had touched her or done something to her, why the fuck would I bring her here to you? I would have just taken her home to my house!' He then shut up and helped me get you out of the car and into the house. I took you into your bedroom and laid you on your bed. Then, as I went to leave, he introduced himself to me properly and told me he was a bit funny about me, our relationship, and how much time we spend together—and that I brought you a new car and now I was dropping you home. He said that was the final straw for him, and he just lost it! To be honest, Ella, I was so close to punching him out and taking you back to my house, but I didn't want you to get in trouble again. It took everything in me to just walk away!"

I thanked him and laughed. "You know, Kevin, you were like a protective big brother-boyfriend last night. I didn't notice it at the ball, but last night you were so cute and protective. I did feel safe, as did the girls. It was just funny seeing you like that. You let me hop in a taxi after the ball, but you didn't let me or my friends take one last night. You're so funny!"

"Yeah, I know ... I didn't want you to hop in that stupid taxi that night at the ball either, but I gave into you back then. I was different then ... We were different then." He paused. "And I couldn't help it. It was really getting to me seeing those guys trying to grind their bodies against yours. It was hard for me to try to relax! But you know, I thought the feeling was bad watching men trying to dry-hump you, but it had nothing on how I felt listening to Robbie shut the front door behind me as I walked to my car ..." I thought I heard fear in his voice.

I didn't know what to say. How do you respond to that? I told him it would have been nice staying at his house and actually spending a night with him, which we had never done before, and then thanked him for listening to me. I told him I wished things could be different, and he agreed with me.

I could see Robbie coming back up towards the house, and I told Kevin I had to go, saying that I would see him first thing Monday morning. I hung up the phone just as Robbie walked back into the house. I slid my body off the bench, leaning my back against it, and slid my phone into the top drawer of the bench behind me.

Robbie entered the room and greeted me. "Good morning— or should I say *afternoon*, my dear! How are we feeling today? Head and feet a bit sore, are they?"

I smiled and nodded. "Yes, it's self-inflicted, I know. I promise you I will not complain!" I went over to the cupboard and pulled out some hydrolytes. I put one into a glass of water and stood there waiting for it to dissolve.

Robbie asked me what I had planned for the day. I told him I wasn't feeling well so I was going to have a lazy day on the couch watching Netflix. He came over to me and told me that sounded great. He thought I needed a downtime day. He told me he was going to have a bite to eat and then head back up to the back paddock and fix the fence. He told me that a tree had come down during the night and had caused a quite a bit of damage to our fence.

He had his lunch and headed back out for the rest of the day as I lay on the couch catching up on a bank of episodes I never had time to watch.

each Days

IT WAS MY job to hang out with Kevin all day, five days a week. And I loved every minute of it. It was always exciting. Every day was a new adventure! It was still surreal that I actually got paid to hang out and have fun with a man who had also become such a big part of my life. He wasn't just my boss or the other man I was sleeping with; he had also become my friend. As the weeks and months rolled over, the appointments and meetings lessened. He would tell me things like, "Hey, Ella, how about we cancel all this morning's appointments and go for a drive somewhere, maybe have a picnic or something!"

On this particular day, it was Kevin's birthday. I had just walked into the office and given him my usual morning greeting kiss and a cuddle. I wished him a happy birthday as I kissed him one more time on his lips. As I pulled my face away from his, I smiled and told him I had birthday present for him. I might have known this man damn well, but what do you buy a man who has everything? Kevin was hard to buy for, almost impossible. I tore my hair out trying to think of something, and it was so hard for me to buy him something and to leave no trace of evidence behind so Robbie couldn't see it or find out.

I passed him a large square gift-wrapped black box and told him to be very careful, not to drop it. He looked so inquisitive as he slowly opened the box. He opened it and looked inside. He seemed so surprised and thrilled by my gift. He couldn't believe I had thought to buy him something like that, he told me. I had bought him a Royal Doulton square crystal whiskey decanter and tumbler set. He told me he absolutely loved it and thanked me as he gave me a kiss and then pulled me to his chest, holding firmly to the back of my head with his hands and while kissing my forehead. When he let go of me, I went back over to my desk.

"Ella, it's going to be a really hot day today, and it's pretty much the last hot day till next summer," he said. "How about we cancel all afternoon appointments and go swimming at Black Rock for the afternoon? They have that gelato place you like there as well."

I laughed and said, "Kevin, I don't have anything to swim in. You know, you really need to start giving me the heads-up so I can bring different clothes to work with me."

"That's okay, baby. You can wear your bra and undies—that always looks sexy! Nah, I'm just kidding. We can go shopping and buy you some!"

I was keen to go to the beach, as he was right. It was going to be a hot day, and as it was late April, it was most likely the last warm day we were going to have for months. We got through all our morning appointments as planned and then headed out together to go shopping. He was so funny to take shopping. We had been shopping in the past for a few things, and I loved it. He would mess around in the shops, picking up bras and holding them against his chest, saying, "Does this suit me? Do I look cute, Ella?" He could always make me laugh. People would stop us while we were out and comment on what a good-looking and happy couple we were.

We drove up to Black Rock and stopped at a local surf shop. We went in to find me a pair of swimmers and Kevin a pair of board shorts. I hadn't been looking through the racks long when I found a gorgeous bikini called the Paradise Bikini in rose gold. It was a pinkish-nude colour and had a natural-style cup compared to the normal fitted or plain bikini top. It contoured to my body perfectly. It came with two different styles of briefs. I liked the ones with the full brief, as I was fit and toned, but I was still more on the curvy side than I was skinny.

As soon as Kevin saw that the swimmers had two options of bottom cuts, I knew which one he would want me to get! He instantly started begging me like an annoying little puppy; he wanted me to get the Brazilian cut bottoms, which were almost a G-String. I had never worn anything like that out in public before. It showed too much flesh for my liking. I tried to explain that to him, but he wouldn't listen or didn't care. He told me, "It's my birthday, so I get what I want, remember!"

The shop assistant couldn't stop laughing at us. She told me, "I wish my husband said things like that to me! Get the Brazilian cut, girl. Give the man what he wants. You only live once, and after all, it is his birthday."

So of course I gave into those devilish brown eyes and we purchased the bottoms he wanted. We also bought a couple towels and a pair of board shorts for Kevin. I swear, you couldn't have wiped the grin off his face if you tried. I asked the shop assistant if I could get changed into the bikinis so I could wear them under my work dress until we reached the beach. She agreed, so we both changed into our swimmers in the change rooms.

After we changed, we went down towards the beach and got a gelato from my favourite shop. I didn't even need to tell him what I wanted to eat anymore. He knew every flavour of the particular foods I like to eat. He ordered for both of us. "Can I please get one cup with one scoop of the coconut and one scoop of chocolate? May I also get another cup with just two scoops of cookies and cream, please?" He passed me the coconut cup as he waited for his cookies and cream.

We walked down to the beach together eating our gelatos and sat on our towels with our feet resting in the sand, watching the waves crash onto the shore in front of us. After we finished our gelatos, I stretched out on my towel, leaning the weight of my body on my elbows, picking up the sand with my feet, and letting the sand granules fall between my toes. I loved the feeling of sand sliding through my feet.

Kevin stood up and put his empty gelato cup on his towel, putting his arm out for me to grab his hand. "Let's do it," he said. I grabbed hold of his hand, and he pulled me off the ground. Kevin was well aware that I was afraid of all water, although the ocean intrigues me and I find it utmost beautiful. I am definitely not a fan of things touching my legs, especially when I cannot see the bottom. He was always so good to me. He held my hand the entire way down to the water and slowly walked me into the water. We continued gradually until the water reached the tops of my hips; then we stopped. He continued to hold my left hand, and we used our free hands to splash each other. I splashed him a good one, and as he wiped the salt water out of his eyes, he couldn't help but smile and laugh at me.

We stopped splashing each other, and he wrapped his arms around me, giving me the firmest hug I think he had ever given me, slowly rocking me side to side. He looked down at me as the waves crashed onto my hips and said, "You know how much I adore you, don't you?" I looked up at him and nodded, slowly kissing him. We were standing under the most perfect blue sky I had ever seen, and I told him, "I wish we could stay in this moment forever!" He agreed and told me that he was having the best day of his life.

For the next couple of hours, we simply went in and out of the water as we pleased, until Kevin looked at his mobile and asked me if I was ready to go. He told me he wanted us to go for a little drive. I nodded and leaned down to grab my towel and rubbish. To be honest, I really didn't care where we went! I always felt so calm and free with Kevin. I believed he brought out a fun side of me that I never even realised I had.

We rinsed off all the sand from our bodies in the freestanding showers up near the car park and then dried ourselves off as we walked up to his car. I asked him if he wanted me to put my clothes back on for wherever we were driving, and he told me "Nah, don't bother. You don't need them where we're going, and you know I love seeing those curves." He didn't care even that my bikini was still slightly damp.

As we started to drive, I noticed we were heading in the direction of his house, and I knew that was exactly where we were going! Kevin said, "Play your favourite song that best describes you. No ... play a song that explains how you are right feeling now."

I laughed at him. "You know, you are so goddam cheesy, Kevin!" I said as I sat back in my chair. I had to think about this. "You are so weird ... but ... I've got it!" I reached into my handbag, got my phone out, and went into my music library, searching for the particular song. I found it and looked over at him, asking, "Are you ready? No judgement now." I clicked PLAY on the song. The beat started to play, and he looked at me and laughed.

"Ella, I couldn't have picked a better song right now. I feel it too! I wish we could!" He turned the volume up and put the windows down, and we both began to yell out the lyrics at each other while he drove, laughing as we sang aloud, dancing our arms out the windows to the flow of the music.

The song I chose was "Fly Away," by Lenny Kravitz, and we both seemed to connect deeply to the song. I wasn't joking. I really did want to fly or run away—I wasn't sure which one, but I couldn't keep this double life up for much longer. I would go from feeling such a high to a crashing low, and it really wasn't good for my health. I didn't realise how unhappy I actually was until I started to feel a constant rush of happiness that I had never felt before with anyone else.

As we pulled up into his driveway, I asked him where Kim was. He said she had gone to the day spa for a facial and then she was off to a Botox party and wouldn't be home for a few hours. I had a giggle to myself. Botox parties! I couldn't think of anything worse—a bunch of rich old bitches lying around drinking French Champagne and getting injections in their faces.

We got out of the car, and as he gave his keys to his private valet driver, he whispered something in his ear. The gentleman replied, "Yes, sir." I will notify you the moment she enters the driveway—you have my word!" I was so happy he did that. I would hate to think what the outcome would be if she found the two of us in their house. Inside the house, all the members of his staff were smiling and nodding their heads towards me. It was kind considering I felt completely embarrassed that I had just walked through his house with wet wavy hair and only wearing a towel wrapped around my body!

I followed him up the stairs to his bedroom. He kept walking until we reached his ensuite bathroom. As I walked through the door, he turned around to face me and held his hand out for me to pass him the towel that was wrapped around my body. I did, and he threw it across the room, landing it in the washing basket. He moved over towards the shower and stopped at the digital screen on the wall. After adjusting the temperature, he turned on the water and just let it run. He came over to me, and using his fingertips, he grabbed the bottom of my bikini top just underneath my breasts. I put my arms straight up in the air, and he pulled my bikini top over my head. He then bent down into a squatting position and slid my bikini bottoms down my legs. After I stepped out of the bottoms one at a time, he stood back up and started to kiss me as he loosened the tied knot on his board shorts. He pushed them off his hips and slid them down his legs, kicking them off his feet.

Kevin held on to my face, thumbs resting on my lower cheeks and his fingertips massaging the skin on the back of my ears as he continued to tilt his head and kiss my lips slowly, sticking his tongue into my mouth and massaging my tongue with his as he walked me backwards into the open shower and positioned me standing underneath the showerhead. Picking me up from behind my thighs, using my arse to hold me up, he pushed me up against the wall of the shower. He continued to kiss me passionately, and then he slowly pulled his face away from mine and smiled. He pinched my chin and put me down until my feet reached the ground, placing me back underneath the water. Stepping out of the shower, he moved to the massage table in the bathroom, off to the side and out of the way. He grabbed the massage oil and headed back towards me as I was standing underneath the showerhead, letting the water hit the top of my head and run down my face.

Joining me, he gently squeezed my breasts. He then leaned down and started to kiss them slowly. He was teasing my nipples with his tongue then began to delicately bite them. I flicked my hair back and stood there with my head leaned back, with my hands held on the back of his head, running my fingers through his hair, holding him firmly in this positon. It felt incredible. I had tingles and sexual pulses running through my entire body. I was so aroused by him and just wanted to have him.

He slowly stopped and looked up at me before fully standing before me. Staring with his smiling eyes, he picked up the bottle of oil he'd set on the floor and squirted it all over me. It smelt like coconut and frangipanis. I turned my body around for him slowly as he sprayed the oil all over me. He then put both his hands on my stomach and started to move his hands, massaging and blending the oil all over my body, all the way down to my toes. He picked me up by my upper thighs and put me up against the wall of the shower, wrapping my legs around his waist. It was so slippery, but my God, was it hot. I squeezed his biceps and massaged my fingertips into his strong, muscular shoulders as I tilted my head to the left and let him kiss my neck. He then put me down and turned my body around, pushing me up against the wall of the shower. I had both hands resting flat against the tiles above my head, holding the weight of my body in this position. I felt him enter me, and then he began to thrust his body behind mine, grabbing my hair, pulling it back, scrunching it in his fingers. He pulled it towards him with one hand and then grabbed one of my breasts, squeezing it in his grip and kissing my tilted neck until we both orgasmed. He whispered in my ear that today had been the best birthday and day he had ever had. He thanked me and kissed me one more time on my lips before sliding himself out of me. I stood there under the water, so relaxed and satisfied.

Kevin started to laugh and picked up a bottle of body wash from the shelf. He squirted me with liquid wash and then poured it all over himself. We started to clean each other with the loofah, spreading the body wash all over each other's bodies. We couldn't help ourselves, and we both started messing around with the body wash, turning his shower into a bubble bath—there was that much foam in the shower. We were collecting the soap in our hands and slapping the soap in each other's face and off our bodies as we continued to laugh and giggle to one another. Once we had rinsed off all of the soap, Kevin turned off the water to the shower and then went to the vanity and grabbed us a couple of towels. I stood there at the edge of the shower as he passed me a towel, then followed him out of his bathroom and into his bedroom.

One of his staff members had brought our belongings in from Kevin's car while we showered. I was so pleased to have my clothes back. We got dressed in his bedroom, which I was sure was as big as my whole house, and then headed out to the balcony. Shortly after sitting down, a woman came out holding a small notepad and asked if we wanted anything to eat or drink. He asked me if I felt like a smoothie, and I nodded and told him "That would be amazing right now!" He then asked for two of his usual oat berry smoothies and a fruit platter. Within what seemed like five minutes, she had already returned with our food and drinks.

We sat there picking at the freshly cut strawberries and cantaloupe, looking out to the majestic view of the sea. It was so beautiful. After we finished our food and drinks, he said, "We'd best start making a move before the crazy bitch gets home!" I agreed with him, and we headed back to the office. As soon as we arrived, I had to go to the bathroom before I went home, as I needed to reapply my make-up, which had washed off at the beach and then later in the shower. I did so and then fixed my hair. As I walked back out to the corridor, Kevin was waiting for me in the office to say goodbye. I kissed him on the lips as I held his face, telling him I would see him tomorrow.

When I arrived home that evening, I felt strange. I felt fine until I walked through the door of our house and saw Robbie. As soon as my eyes met his, I immediately felt sick to my stomach. The strangest thing was that he hadn't actually done anything wrong. I felt almost overwhelmed! I had experienced one of the best days of my life to date, yet I had this feeling. Emotion is a feeling that I had never been in touch with in the past, but for some reason, I felt as if I could cry or needed to cry. My heart was racing, my hands were shaking, and I thought I might vomit. I tried desperately to ignore it.

As it was a mild night as far as temperature, I decided we would have a barbecue, with easy chargrilled mixed vegetables for me and steak and grilled vegetables for Robbie. I stood at the bench and started to prepare dinner, and as I was slicing the vegetables, I had so many thoughts going through my mind concerning my life, Kevin, Robbie, who I was, and who I wanted to be.

Robbie came into the house with a bunch of daisies and set them down next to me on the kitchen counter, telling me he had picked them for me from the meadow. Robbie had walked past the same meadow daily for the past four years at least, and he never had previously thought of doing that for me! I felt I should be grateful for the flowers, but I was more concerned what his agenda was. I had learned in the past year or so that Robbie didn't do anything without getting something in return.

He then creeped up behind me and moved my hair to one side of my neck. He whispered in my ear, "I've been thinking maybe we should try IVF. It's been a while and still nothing!" There it was! My anxiety reached its peak at that exact point, and my hands started to shake uncontrollably as I continued to try to slice the vegetables with a knife. My vision started to go blurry, and I was utterly speechless. He continued to talk about the subject. My hearing was coming in and out, echoing as if I were standing in a tunnel.

"A few of the guys at work have been through it with their wives. I think we should look into it," I heard Robbie say faintly, as the reverberations in my head were incredibly loud. I calmly placed the knife on the chopping board and turned around to face him. He kept rambling on about the subject, and I just lost total control of my body and snapped at him.

"I have told you so many times that I'm not ready! You promised me, Robbie, that you would stop pressuring me. I can't cope with this right now!" I told him in a stern voice, my body and voice shaking as my anxiety levels went completely out of control. In my whole life, I had never felt as I did right at that moment. I started to cry uncontrollably. I could tell by the look on Robbie's face that he was shocked, as he had never seen me cry in the entire time we had dated and been married! I had my hands over my face, and my body just let it out. I fell to my knees and told Robbie as I wept, "I can't do this anymore. I can't be the person you want me to be anymore! I just can't do it anymore. This has to stop. I have nothing left in me to give you. I want a divorce, Robbie!"

Robbie became extremely defensive. He picked up the flowers he had just picked for me and threw them against the wall, smashing them. He started pacing up and down the kitchen, ranting and raving about my hormones and shouting that it was my fault that I had given up on us.

As I sobbed on the floor, leaning my body against the island bench, hitting my head repeatedly against the cupboard doors behind me, I told him that I had to leave. I couldn't be in this prison of a life anymore! He walked up to me, squatted down to my height, and glared into my eyes. I remembered seeing this same look in his eyes after the ball. He grabbed my wrist and squeezed it so tightly that it started to turn red. I could feel a burning sensation in my wrist. I could tell he was hurting me, but I had so many sensations flowing throughout my body that I actually couldn't feel the pain of what he was doing to me. Since I was not reacting to him, he started to grind his teeth and then squeezed his hands harder.

"You're not going anywhere! I told you that!" he exclaimed. I just stared blankly back at him, feeling completely naked. He let go of my wrist, stood up, grabbed his cigarettes and his beer, and stomped outside, slamming the flywire door on his way out.

I realised that everything in the past year had finally caught up with me. The double life I had been living had finally become too much. I couldn't be the wife Robbie wanted, and I couldn't be Kevin's mistress anymore! They were both playing tug of war with my body and mind, and it had finally caught up with me. I always knew it had to end. Eventually, my body and my mind just couldn't cope anymore. They had both had enough!

I sat on the floor for the next hour, sobbing to myself and visualising grabbing my bag and car keys, going for a drive and never coming back, starting again somewhere else, far, far away, starting a fresh new life. In that moment, I wanted to run for the hills from both of the men in my life; the extreme highs and lows between the two were exhausting. I felt as if I were drowning and couldn't reach a hand to save me. My body felt simply depleted. I had do something. I couldn't keep going on like this.

I lay awake for hours that night with hundreds of thoughts rushing through my mind. I had to come up with a game plan. I ran through every scenario in my mind. I knew I couldn't leave Robbie. He would kill me, especially if I tried to leave him for another man. It would also put the other man's life in jeopardy. I couldn't do that either! Robbie was no longer the same man I married. He was once a kind man, a man I thought would one day make a wonderful father. Now he treated me more like he was my prison guard than my husband, and Kevin made me so happy but had never made mention of leaving Kim. I think that is why I wanted to run away; it simply felt like it would be the easiest way.

In a strange way, it was funny how only a few hours prior, I was having the best day of my life, lying peacefully on the beach and then making love to an incredible man in his shower. Then, only hours later, I was having an emotional breakdown and wanting to run away from everything, to try to get away from them both. I remember thinking as the waves crashed up against my hips that I could have died in that moment, in Kevin's arms, as his eyes gazed into mine, and had no regrets. But I did believe that as much as I adored my time with Kevin, my relationship with him as his mistress was really bad for my health. I would feel incredibly happy, on cloud nine, one moment, and then I would come home to Robbie and that feeling would come crashing down, as it was the complete opposite. My husband only noticed my existence when he was hungry or, these days, wanting to make a baby. I still didn't trust him and his temper. I had to stop myself from telling him the truth tonight—that it wasn't that I didn't necessarily want a baby, but that I just I don't want to have his baby! I refuse to bring a child into this world because they were a means to control their mother, and especially not with a man with his appalling traits.

I didn't want my future child to inherit or learn his temper and personality. After hours of back and forth in my mind, I finally made my decision.

CHAPTER 13

*J*ealously Is a Curse

THE NEXT DAY, we woke as usual to our alarms. I got out of bed and helped Robbie get ready for work. I acted as if nothing had happened the night before and kissed him goodbye, sending him on his way. As he went to leave for work, Robbie stood at the front door, looked back at me, and said, "I will see you tonight, Ella!"

I nodded and said, "Of course." He smiled and left.

I would normally go for a run and then do Pilates, but this morning I had something more important to do. I went to my handbag and grabbed iPad, going into Microsoft Word. I checked over what I had written and was happy with it, so I pressed the print button and then collected it off my printer in my office. I signed the bottom, folding the paper in half, and then placed it in my handbag. I walked to the bathroom and then jumped into shower. I was quickly trying to get ready for work, as the document had taken longer than anticipated and now I was running slightly late.

When I got to work, Kevin was more excited than usual to see me. He gave me a greeting kiss, holding my face with both his hands, and told me, "You won't believe what I did this morning!"

The phone rang, and I apologised to him and told him I had to answer it. After the conversation, I hung up the phone and let Kevin know that something had gone down overnight and an emergency meeting had been called for all of the forty-three, now forty-four members, including me, and it was to start in only thirty minutes' time. We urgently grabbed our stuff and rushed to the car.

He sped the entire way across town until we made it to the office building where we had the usual monthly meeting. As soon as we walked in, we saw all the members fighting, yelling, blaming, and pushing each other. Kevin immediately wolf-whistled and brought the whole room to silence. "That's enough! What the hell is going on?" he shouted.

James, one of the members, started to explain, seeming frazzled. "There's been a leak. Johnny blabbed. He told the media everything about the deals we had made for next month!"

"Everyone sit down. We will sort this out," Kevin said politely.

For the next two hours, Kevin tried to keep everyone in good spirits. I let Kevin know during the meeting that I was going to organise food and drinks, as I could see it was going to be a long day. I got up and went out into the waiting room in the corridor, where all of the other personal assistants waited. As I tried to get their attention, I saw them all sitting in their seats giving me filthy looks.

I told them, "I know you all don't like me, but it's not about me. It's going to be a long day for everyone, so I suggest we all work together. I need someone to organise platters of food for the guys so they can all pick at the food as they talk. Keep the coffees coming and get yourselves food and something to drink!"

Surprisingly everyone nodded and then started working together. They started mingling with one another, working out who was ordering and doing what. Within twenty minutes, the coffees and platters started rolling in. The members were so delighted, and their moods started to shift slowly. It ended up taking the whole day to sort out, but Kevin ended up coming up with a solution to all their problems.

We were exhausted after the long day we had had. We pulled back into the car park back at our office, and I told Kevin I needed to go to the bathroom, saying that I needed to go back inside. He told me he was done for the night and leaned in to give me a kiss goodbye. I was so exhausted, and I knew it wasn't the right time, but I did it anyway. I reached into my handbag and took out the document I had typed only that morning. I could see the emotions on his face change as he read it.

To whom it may concern,

Today, 28 April, I would like to give notice of two weeks. I am grateful for the position and opportunity I have been given. I regret to inform you that I will finish up on the 12 May.

Ella Jade Moore

He scrunched up the letter and held it firmly in his fist. He looked over at me with disappointment. Then that look turned into one of betrayal. "What's going on, babe? We had an amazing day yesterday. To be honest, it was one of the best days of my life so far! And now, today, you're leaving me. I don't understand what's going through your head." He put his hand on my lap and softly massaged my inner thigh.

I began to cry. "I can't do this anymore, Kevin … I'm sorry! I just can't handle living like this anymore. I feel as if I have schizophrenia. This double life is too much for me! I refuse to be a boring housewife to Robbie and be your mistress. My mind just can't cope anymore!" I sobbed, looking down at the floor of his car.

"Please, Ella, don't do this … I love you! I'd do anything for you. You know that," he said as he started to get teary.

"I am so sorry, Kevin!" I leaned over and put my hand on his face, rubbing his cheekbone. I kissed his forehead and then moved my lips to meet his lips and kissed him. I turned around, grabbed my handbag, and got out of his car.

He tried to grab my hand and yelled out to me, "Wait! Please, Ella, I had something I needed to tell you!" He begged me to stop and listen to what he had to say, but I refused.

"Not now, Kevin. I can't! I'm so sorry."

I was too quick. He couldn't secure his grip on my hand, and he let go. I quickly shut his car door and started walking towards the entry door to get back into the building. Kevin sat in his car watching me until I reached the door. I turned around and looked back at him. He turned back away from me, held his foot on the accelerator and pulled the handbrake, burning the rubber on his tyres in front of me in the car park, skating his car all over the place, leaving rubber rings on the tarred ground. I knew he was so hurt. I had never seen him like this before, but I didn't know what else to do. I had to make a stand!

I walked into the building and made my way to the bathroom. Once I had finished, I began walking back to the car park. As I went past Heather's desk, I saw her packing up for the day, as it was her knock-off time. I wished her a goodnight, and she replied, "Yeah, you too!" I had almost reached the door of the car park when I heard, "Hey, Ella, wait. Before you go, I really want to tell you something. Did ever wonder how you got the job with Kevin to begin with?"

My ears perked up, and I paused. "Well, I can explain it to you if you like." I turned around to face her. "A couple of weeks before you started with Kevin, he asked me to contact the HR department, as he wanted a copy of every current employee's file! I thought it was strange at the time, considering he had never requested anything of the sort or taken an interest in the staff previously. Did you ever wonder how you got the top PA job in the company without any experience? He tracked you down, Ella. You must have caught his eye. You could call it stalking if you like. Once he found you, he asked me to make a copy of your file and return it to him immediately. I'm a snoop and couldn't help myself. I had to check you out. He then had to make a position available for you. So his long-time assistant, Kristine, got fired to make way for you! I have worked for Kevin for a long time. I must admit that I thought once he got what he wanted from you, he would have given you the flick, like every other bimbo he has screwed in the past. But he didn't! I just thought you should know that he wanted you from the get-go. Kevin always gets what he wants, and he will eventually get bored and tired of you—he always does!"

Heather had a sense of delight to her voice as she told me this. I could tell that she was extremely jealous of my relationship with Kevin; however, as much as she couldn't stand me, I did believe she was telling me the truth. I didn't actually know what to say in response, so I brushed her off and told her I would see her tomorrow. As I walked out to the car park, I couldn't help but think about what Heather had just told me. I might be blonde, but I have never been stupid! Of course, I knew that I got the job because Kevin admired me.

I got into my car and started to drive home. I had Heather running through my mind in addition to Kevin and the look he had given me before I got out of his car. He'd told me he loved me for the first time, and I didn't even say it back to him! I just shut the door on him.

I called Robbie on my way home to find out if we needed anything at home, as I was stopping at the shops. As unhappy as I was, for some reason, I just carried on with the same daily routines. He told me that we were out of muesli bars and he needed more cigarettes, asking me if I would mind grabbing them for him. I went into the shops and grabbed a couple pieces of fruit, muesli bars, and the stinking cigarettes for Robbie as he requested.

As I walked towards my car, I thought I heard footsteps. I quickly stopped, but there was no one around. The shops were completely empty and it was so dark that I couldn't really see anything. I thought I must had been hearing things and continued to put the groceries in the boot of my car. All of a sudden, I heard footsteps right behind me. I turned my body around to see what it was …

Whack! Everything went black, and I fell to the ground. I started to come in and out of consciousness and could feel an excruciating pulsing pain to the back of my head. My body felt weightless as my body was being dragged by my arms from behind me, through the car park, and as my vision came in and out, I watched my dragging feet get farther and farther away from my car. Everything was like a dream. I could hear people talking but couldn't understand what they were saying because of the loud ringing in my ears. My vision was coming in and out, and I could feel my eyes starting to close again. My head was getting heavy, and I was trying with all my strength to force my eyes to open. I could hear Oprah in my head, saying, "Don't let them take you from point A to point B," but I could only slightly see with my eyes only open about a millimetre.

My body was being thrown in the boot of a car, and I couldn't do anything in my power to stop it. I was trying to get some movement in my body. As I lay there, I could hear voices echoing, talking to each other as if we were in a tunnel. I felt something pushed up against my mouth and nose. I could smell heavy chemicals and realised they had were holding a cloth of turpentine or something against my face. I tried to fight, but I felt a sudden rush to my head and then everything went black.

CHAPTER 14

Detective Sergeant Andersen

AFTER I HADN'T arrived home, Robbie waited around for two hours after trying to call my phone over forty times. Robbie decided to call the local police station. He told them I was on my way home from work and that he had spoken to me. I was stopping at the shops and then coming straight home and that he was extremely worried for my welfare. The officer asked Robbie where I usually stopped on my way home and said that they would check it out and get back to him.

Within the hour, a police officer had called Robbie and asked him to come down to the station and to bring along the most recent photo he had of me. Robbie jumped straight in the car and headed down to the station. When he arrived, he told the officer who greeted him at the front desk his name and told the officer he been asked to come down. The officer went out the back and returned with another officer, who introduced himself as Detective Sergeant Andersen. He shook Robbie's hand and said, "Nice to meet you, Robert. Could you please follow me to the interview room so we can talk in private?"

Robbie followed the detective into the interview room and handed the officer the photo he had requested. He asked Robbie to sit down. He then explained to him that they had found my car and that the car was still parked at the shopping centre with the boot completely left open, with all the shopping untouched inside. He went on to say, "We found your wife's handbag on the ground near her car at the scene. It had been dropped and was lying on its side with some of the contents on the ground, which tells us, Robert, that your wife may have run into a struggle." He asked Robbie if he could have a look at his phone to check and confirm the time and length of the last conversation he had had with me. The officer told Robbie that my disappearance was now suspicious and that it had been listed as a missing person's case. They were collecting the security footage as they spoke.

"I have a few questions I need to ask you," he said to Robbie. First of all, is there anyone who would want to hurt your wife … or did she have any enemies you were aware of?"

Robbie seemed distressed and told the officer, "She has always caught the eye of every man. She doesn't have any enemies, though. She has always kept to herself. She doesn't go out enough or see anyone much to have enemies, but she does spend too much time with her boss. You might want to check him out. His name is Kevin Jacobs!" The officer started to jot on his notepad.

"Since you mention this Kevin character, I would like to know how your marriage was."

Robbie started to get defensive towards the sergeant. "Our marriage was fine! Everyone has their ups and downs. What's that have to do with anything? Someone has taken my wife!"

"I have to ask these questions, Robert, so I can ascertain what has happened and where your wife is. It's critical to your wife's welfare that you answer honestly, as the sooner I discover what is going on, the sooner I can bring your wife home to you!" the sergeant told Robbie in a stern voice as he moved closer to intimidate him.

Robbie sat there and refused to answer any more questions. Sergeant Andersen stood up, shook Robbie's hand firmly, and told him, "We will do our best to try to find your wife. I'll keep you updated. If you think of anything else, here's my card. Please call me."

Robbie stood up and made his way to the door. The officer said, "Wait, before you go, we found Ella's phone in her handbag and are unable to unlock it, as it has a swipe pattern. Could you please unlock it for me?" Robbie grabbed the phone from the officer and unlocked it. The officer snatched back the phone quickly, with Robbie trying to sneak a look at it. He told Robbie, "I'm just having a look through her call list. She seems to have fifty-two recent missed calls—forty-nine from you and three from a 'Kevin'—as well as one text message." The officer opened the text message from Kevin. It read, "I've tried to call you a few times. Can you please answer your phone! You're probably in the middle of cooking dinner. I just wanted to speak to you about what happened today. Call me, please, if you get a chance, Ella. Otherwise, I'll see you tomorrow!"

As Sergeant Andersen read the message aloud, Robbie shook his head in disgust. When he had finished reading the message, Robbie said, "I can't stand that prick at all!"

"Yes, okay. Sorry about that, Robert. We'll be in touch!" Sergeant Andersen moved the phone away from Robbie and placed it in the pocket of his jacket. Robbie left the station and returned home.

Sergeant Andersen then called Kevin using the number in my phone and asked him if could come down to the station. Within the hour, Kevin arrived at the station. He told the officers his name and asked them what it was regarding. Sergeant

Andersen asked Kevin to follow him into the interview room so they could speak in private. As they went into the room, they both sat down facing one another. The officer placed a photo of me on the table and slid it in front of Kevin. Andersen immediately started to question him.

"Kevin, could you please tell me the last time you saw or heard from Mrs. Ella Jade Moore?"

Kevin got out of his seat and started pacing the room back and forth, stressing, pulling on his hair, and then frantically saying, "What did he do to her? Please tell me she is okay. Please tell me she is okay!" He started to cry and hold on to his head.

The officer asked him to please remain seated and then let him know, "Ella Jade Moore has gone missing. Her husband was the one who alerted us that she hadn't made it home! Her car was left suspiciously abandoned in the Olive Grove Mall tonight, and we are trying to get to the bottom of this."

Kevin seemed utterly devastated. "My poor Ella is missing," he continued repeating.

The officer said to Kevin, "Before, you mentioned someone could have done something to her! Who were you referring to, Kevin?"

"Her husband, Robbie!" he swiftly answered.

The officer started to interrogate Kevin. "What makes you think that he would do anything to hurt his wife? He seemed genuinely concerned for her welfare."

"Because he's crazy. He has hurt her in the past. He can be controlling and abusive!" said Kevin.

"Could you please explain your relationship with Ella Jade Moore to me, please?" questioned Sergeant Andersen.

"Ella Jade is my assistant, and she has worked for me the past twelve months or so. She works by my side, all day, five days a week. We are very close!" Kevin replied, stressed, as the officer slid the photo side to side on the table in front of Kevin.

Kevin picked up the photo and just held it, staring at it as he continued to sob.

"I have been around traps, Kevin. I am not a silly man by any stretch. Can you please tell me when you first started sleeping with Mrs. Moore!"

Kevin started to play with the photo and wipe his fingers over it. He replied, "I'm not. We are just really close and she tells me these things!"

Sergeant Andersen took a deep breath and sighed. "From what I've heard, Ella was a pretty private person and didn't really talk to anyone. Kevin, you were the last person to see her, and if you are keeping something from me, I will get to the bottom of it!" said Sergeant Andersen. He told Kevin he could leave and that they would be in touch.

"Oh, wait, Kevin. Before you go, one last question. What happened today between the two of you?"

"What makes you think anything happened today between us?" asked Kevin.

"I have her phone. You tried to call her three times and then you sent her a message, telling her she needed to call you about what happened today."

Kevin replied, "We had a pretty full-on day with meetings, and I was just checking how she was feeling! That's all." Kevin could tell that Andersen didn't believe a word he was saying, and he just waited for a response from the detective.

"You know, as her employer, you seem more upset that she is missing than her own husband does! Either you are in love with her or you are involved in her disappearance. I will find out exactly what is going on. You may leave for now; we'll be in touch!"

Kevin left the station and drove directly to my house. He knocked on the door. When Robbie opened the door, Kevin immediately charged into the house with force, grabbing

Robbie's throat and forcing the door open. Kevin started yelling at him. "What did you do to her? Tell me what did you do to her! Where is she?" Kevin threw Robbie against the wall, still holding him, choking him in his rage. Robbie tried to fight back to protect himself, but Kevin was too strong for him.

Robbie dropped his legs in self-defence, and they both fell to the ground, punching each other. Robbie was struggling and trying desperately to speak. "I didn't touch her!" he said, gasping for air. He loosened Kevin's grip and repeated, "I didn't touch her. I swear I don't know where she is!"

"I swear, Robbie, if you have done anything to her, I will come back for you! I promise you that!" threatened Kevin. Kevin let go of his throat, stood up, and left the house.

One hour later …

When Kevin arrived home, he headed straight into the lounge and poured himself a Scotch from the decanter. He picked up his glass and took his first sip. Hearing the doorbell sound, he looked down at his Rolex on his left wrist and checked for the time. He seemed surprised to have a visitor this late in the evening. He opened the front door. "Sergeant Andersen, how can I help you? Long time no see!" said Kevin sarcastically.

"Kevin, may we please come in?" asked Sergeant Andersen, standing at the door with another officer. Kevin opened the door wide and let the officers in, already starting to walk away. They shut the door behind them and followed Kevin as he went back into his lounge. He showed them where to sit and then offered them both a drink of Scotch. They politely declined his offer, and the two officers sit down on the three-seater couch. Kevin sat down on the couch opposite them.

"Kevin, I received a phone call from Mr. Robert Moore not long after you left the station tonight. He's accusing you of going to his house tonight and assaulting him. Is this true?" asked Sergeant Andersen.

"Yes, it is!" Kevin answered brazenly as he took a gulp of his Scotch. He watched the drink in his glass move from side to side.

"Why did you go over to see Mr. Moore? It's my job to find Ella, not yours!"

Kevin bluntly ignored Sergeant Andersen.

"I am going to ask you again, Kevin, and this time don't lie to me. What is your relationship with Mrs. Moore!"

Kevin just sat there dazed, drinking his Scotch.

"Kevin, I'm not stupid. No one is this distraught or angry over a colleague. I know it has to be personal! What is your relationship with her?" Sergeant Andersen demanded.

Kevin took the last sip of his drink, stood up, and poured himself another Scotch. Then he started to explain to the officers as he continued to walk the length of the room. "It was around five months ago—I remember the first time it happened; it was the day after my charity ball. Please … this has to be off the record. He cannot find out. He will kill her … if he hasn't already." Kevin's stress levels started to increase as he gave them more information. "If she's dead, it's my fault! I should have just left it alone. But I couldn't help myself. We have such a powerful chemistry. I have never felt the way I do for her for anyone in my life!"

Sergeant Andersen asked Kevin, "How do you know Robert has hurt his wife in the past? Is that something she confided in you?"

"No, she came into the office wearing the evidence, and she was wearing so much make-up to try to cover up the bruises, but I could see how swollen her face was underneath. That was the first day we ever did anything. I was comforting her, and it just happened," Kevin explained.

"If her husband is as bad as you say, why didn't she just leave him?" asked the officer.

"Because she was scared he would kill her. I think she felt she had no choice, and I, regrettably, never offered her any other solutions because I am an idiot!" said Kevin.

"Is there anything else you can tell me? You spend a lot of time with her. Is there anyone else who would want to hurt her?" asked the officer.

"No, she didn't really have anyone. She has a couple of friends, Kristina and Sophie. They seem to be her family, as she has no family except for one brother who lives interstate. Other than that, she didn't really talk about anyone else."

"Okay, thank you for telling me the truth. I had a feeling something was going on between the two of you. When I looked Ella up, I did find out that she had been stalked in the past and had two restraining orders on ex-boyfriends. Did she ever mention anything to you?"

"No, she didn't. You don't think …?" Kevin seemed rather confused and worried.

"I'm not sure. I'm trying to work out the secret life of Mrs. Moore. It's proving to be one of my most complex cases to date! Now, on a different subject, you have to stay away from Mr. Moore. I could charge you right now with assault, but I'm not going to at this stage if you promise me that you will stay away from him. But the moment you go anywhere near him, I cannot protect you! Do you understand, Kevin?"

Kevin agreed and promised the sergeant he would stay away. Both officers then left for the evening.

The next morning, Kevin went to work as usual. As soon as he arrived, he sat down at his desk and called Heather into his office. He asked her to cancel all the appointments for the next two days, which I had previously scheduled for him, and then declared that he didn't want to see anyone. She was to take messages ongoing, until he said otherwise. He grabbed his coat and left the building for the day. He went home to speak to Kim, but when he got there, he couldn't find her. He spoke to his house staff, and they told him that Kim wasn't there. He called her phone, but she didn't answer, so he left a message on her voice mail: "Kim, it's me … Have you thought about what we spoke about yesterday? Could you get back to me as soon as possible, please? I just want to get it over and done with!"

He grabbed his keys and headed back out. As he drove around, he decided to stop at CC and Co Tavern, where we had our night out. He went inside and ordered himself a straight Scotch and sat slumped over at the bar, drinking all afternoon. There was a television hanging from the ceiling in the corner of the bar. The five o'clock news came on, and he was watching the television and swishing his Scotch around the glass at the same time when a news story came on that got his attention. Robbie was on the news with Sergeant Andersen, holding a photo of me, begging the public's help to try to find me. He rushed down the rest of his drink and slammed the glass on the bar, threw down a couple hundred dollar notes on the bar, and then grabbed his coat and headed for his car. He hopped into his car and tried to call Kim again. Once again, it rang out. He then rang Heather at the office, and the phone rang out. Kevin started to become extremely frustrated at the situation and threw his phone at his glovebox. "Why isn't any one answering their fucking phones?" he shouted aloud.

He then called Sergeant Andersen and asked him if there were any updates in the case. "I really cannot give you any information, Kevin. You're not family or her partner—you are just her lover. It doesn't entitle you to any information."

"Please … I beg you! I'm going crazy! Please just give me something," Kevin pleaded, wanting Sergeant Andersen to give him anything to put his mind at ease.

"Look, I really shouldn't do this, but we have played the CT footage, and it does show Ella putting the shopping into the boot of her car, and then we can see one person creeping up behind her. She was struck from behind, her head hit with a tyre iron, and then another person with a slightly shorter build helped that person drag her body across the car park to another car. Then they both shoved her into the boot of their vehicle. We have a specialist working on it right now, trying to decipher the bumper sticker on the vehicle, as they had taken off the plates of the car, and make out the description of the kidnappers as well."

"Are you serious? I don't understand who on earth would want to hurt her!" Kevin said as he began to weep. He thanked him and then hung up the phone. After the call ended, his phone rang immediately. It was Kim. He answered the phone. Kim sounded distressed and told him she needed more time and needed to sort it out in her head before she made the next step. He agreed and told her he wanted to deal with the situation promptly and to not to take too long in her decision because the arrangement won't hold up.

Robbie went home after the press conference. A couple of hours had passed by, and he had just spent the afternoon drinking while slouched on the couch. He got up and grabbed himself another beer from the fridge, and that's when he heard the front doorbell sound. It was Sergeant Andersen, and he was holding a piece of paper. "I am sorry to do this to you, Robbie, but I have a search warrant to search your home for any clues in your wife's disappearance."

Robbie seemed shocked. "How did you get a warrant? You must have found something on me to get a warrant approved!"

"I'm sorry, Robbie, but I have two sources telling me that you were a controlling and possessive husband, and one source has said that Ella was considering a divorce. Your body matches the description of one of the kidnappers in the footage we have …

and you were the last person to speak to her. Unfortunately, it makes you the main suspect!"

Robbie snatched the piece of paper out of his hands as Sergeant Andersen pushed the door open for the others officers to enter. As they went through the house, room by room, Robbie yelled out to them, "I have nothing to hide, you know! Go for your lives!"

The officers continued to walk into the house and started going through all of our belongings, opening every drawer and pulling everything apart. The house looked like a bomb had gone off. Robbie sat outside on the porch the entire time, sipping on beer and smoking his cigarettes. The search went on for over an hour. Finally, one of the officers came over to Sergeant Andersen and said, "Sir, we may have found something." Andersen told Robbie to remain seated and followed the officer into the bathroom. Robbie genuinely seemed shocked; he couldn't work out what they might have found.

Sergeant Andersen was in the bathroom for a few minutes talking to the other officers, and then he returned and informed Robbie as to what they had found. "Robbie, did you know your wife was pregnant?" questioned Sergeant Andersen.

Robbie looked stunned. "No!" he answered, shocked. "No! She honestly hadn't said a word. I don't really know how she could be. I've been pushing her for a baby for a very long time, and she wouldn't have a bar of it. She's been fighting me on this subject for months!"

Sergeant Andersen sat down next to Robbie. "I'm sorry, but I need to inform you that your wife has been having an affair with her employer, Kevin Jacobs, and there's a chance it could be his baby."

Robbie stood up and threw his half-empty beer bottle, smashing it all over the paved tiles in the patio. Sergeant Andersen grabbed him by the shoulders, as his rage was becoming explosive, and yelled at him to keep it together. The officers told Robbie that they had finished their search and would now be leaving for the evening. They apologised for any inconvenience caused.

Sergeant Andersen got into his car and drove straight to Kevin's house. He knocked on the door, and one of Kevin's staff members let him know that Kevin was not yet home, telling him that he would let him know the moment he returned home.

Kevin arrived home late that evening and stumbled out of his car, starting to stagger his way to his front door. When he heard a noise, he swiftly turned around to see what it was. He saw Sergeant Andersen standing in the pitch-dark waiting for him. He told him there was news with the investigation and he needed to speak to him urgently in private, asking if they could go inside the house to discuss the subject further. Kevin seemed drunk, and Andersen could immediately tell that he was heavily intoxicated. As they went into the house, he drilled him on how much he had to drink, considering he had just witnessed him get out of a vehicle he was driving. Kevin shrugged him off and replied, "Only a couple! You only saw me on private property; same rules don't apply!" He made his way towards the lounge. He poured himself a water and asked Sergeant Andersen if he would like one as well.

He declined and said, "I need to inform you of an update with the investigation."

Kevin seemed scared about what Sergeant Andersen was about to tell him. "Please tell me you've found her alive!" he said, fearing the worst.

"We haven't found her as of yet, Kevin. Earlier this evening, we searched her home for any clues and evidence that could assist us with her disappearance, and we found two massive pieces to this puzzle, which I would like to talk to you about."

"What did you find?" asked Kevin.

"Firstly, we found a pregnancy test in the rubbish bin of their bathroom en suite. It was positive. Were you aware Ella was pregnant?" questioned Andersen.

Kevin put his head back into the chair and said, "I had no idea. I wish she had told me! I would have been supportive! You have told Robbie about the baby and our affair, haven't you?" he asked with a smirk.

Andersen replied, "I had to; it's part of the investigation."

"How did my mate take the news?" He chuckled to himself and then got up from the couch and poured himself a Scotch, which he sculled down.

"He took it like any man finding out his missing wife was having an affair … and could be pregnant from another man! How do you think, Kevin?" Andersen replied sarcastically.

"What was the other thing you found?" Kevin asked.

"We had our tech team go through her phone, iPad, and laptop to find her most recent activity log. They found something on the same day Ella went missing. She had typed a resignation letter to you, giving you two weeks' notice! It was dated the twenty-eighth of April, yesterday's date. So, Kevin, we have a rich, married, powerful man who is having an affair with his assistant …who is also married. She gets knocked up and tells you. You don't want her to keep the baby. She resigns to leave and runs away with the baby and … then you decide to kill her—and your tears are nothing but guilt! Is that what happened, Kevin?"

Kevin poured himself another Scotch and shrugged his shoulders.

"You are an intelligent man, Kevin! I shouldn't have to remind you not to go too far now. No taking any holidays right now. You have moved up to the most suspicious suspect in Ella Jade's disappearance!"

"I know you don't think much of me, and I know how it looks! If I were in your position, with the timeline, events, the facts and evidence, it all points to me. I can see that myself, but I am honestly in love with Ella. I could never harm her! We spent the day together the day before she disappeared. It was the best day of my life, and I had already before that day made up my mind, but it just reiterated what needed to happen. The next day, I tried to tell her, but we got stuck in a meeting all day and I didn't get a chance. When we returned to the office car park, I was exhausted and I dropped her at her car. I told her I was just going to go home, but then something changed when I stopped the car. She began to cry, which I had never seen before. I tried to comfort her, and then she handed me her resignation letter and told me she couldn't live the double life anymore. I tried to tell her what I had done, but she wouldn't hear me, and she got out of my car. I got so angry that I did a couple burnouts in the rooftop car park. Then I left. That was the last time I laid eyes on her! You have me completely misunderstood. My tears are regret, not guilt!" Kevin explained.

"What did you try to tell her!" questioned Sergeant Andersen.

"I tried to tell her that I had asked Kim for a divorce. I wanted to be with Ella; I wanted to start a family with her! I would give everything I owned to spend my life with that woman," Kevin explained.

"That sounds like a cute story, but I don't know how it will hold up in court. It's honestly not looking very good for you! I do partially believe you, but I still feel like there's something not quite right. I just can't figure out what it is."

Kevin remained silent and stared at Andersen, knowing that everything he was saying was the truth. It did look terribly bad on his behalf.

"So, married Kevin, I can't imagine your wife was pleased to hear you wanted a divorce! Did she know about your affair with Ella? Did she know she could be pregnant by you?" asked Andersen.

"My wife and I have an arrangement. I have been sleeping with other women for years, and she has never cared! She didn't know about my relationship with Ella. We were discreet, and *no*, she didn't know Ella was pregnant, just as I didn't know until five minutes ago either!" Kevin was beginning to get extremely frustrated with Sergeant Andersen.

Andersen asked him where his wife was. Kevin told him, "I never actually know where Kim is, and I don't really care either!" He threw his hands up in the air and then reached into his jacket pocket. He pulled out a notepad and wrote Kim's mobile number on it. He passed it to Sergeant Andersen and told him to go ahead and call her. "I don't give a shit. Tell her Ella's pregnant while you're at it! I just want Ella to back come back home alive!"

Andersen took the piece of paper with the number and told him they would be in touch.

CHAPTER 15

Cold and Alone

I GRADUALLY OPENED my eyes and could instantly feel a massive migraine. My head was pulsating and throbbing. I was in excruciating pain and finding it hard to breathe. I felt as if I were hung-over, as if had drunk a litre of vodka and lived to tell the tale. I moved my hands to feel my head and realised they were tied behind my back and that I had a cotton gag tied tightly around my head to block my mouth. I slightly moved my head and hands to try to have a look behind me and then noticed that my hands were tied so tight with cable ties that they were cutting into my wrists and causing them to bleed. My head felt itchy. I could feel a tight dry-like paste on my temple. I leaned over and wiped my forehead onto my knee to see what it was. I had wiped my own blood over my ripped stockings. My beautiful leather shoes were scuffed all over, my stockings had tears and dirt on them and were only just holding onto my legs, and I had cuts all over my legs as if I had been dragged on the ground. My body was beyond freezing, and I was sitting on a cold, damp floor in a concrete room. I could see the steam moving from my mouth through my gag out to the air; the temperature was that cold. There was only one window I could see, on the far left wall of the room. It was small, but it was big enough to see that daylight was shining into the room, which made me realise that I had been in this room overnight. I started to scream for help, but with the gag, it was pointless. No one could hear me; it was just muffled noise. I tried to bite my way through the gag, but it was exhausting and I almost run out of breath. The gag was blocking part of my nose, making it almost impossible to breathe.

I tried to get up off the ground, but the cable ties were threaded through another cable that was linked to a pipe that ran up the wall. I rattled the pipe to try to free my hands but had no luck. I became so frustrated. I just sat there rattling my hands with force, trying to cry out for help. I caused so much more damage to my hands in doing so, but I was so emotional that I didn't care. I had been sitting in this room for hours and hadn't even heard a bird or anything. It was dead quiet! I could smell dried hay and horse manure, and I had no idea where I was, other than on someone's rural property. I knew I was far enough away that no one could hear me. I kept trying to yell out through the gag. It was just muffled noise and a complete waste of my energy! Even if someone did hear me, no one would know what the noise was.

I couldn't help but wonder if anyone was even looking for me. Two nights ago, I had basically told Robbie I wanted to leave him. As far as Kevin, yesterday I broke up with him as well and had only told Kevin two days ago, after the beach, that I wanted to run away. Would they even realise I was missing or would they think I had just taken off—or did one of them put me here? It would be my karma, I guess, for being a shitty cheating wife. I had so many thoughts about what I was doing here and who may have put me here. I continued to sit on the cold ground with all the thoughts exploding in my mind as

I shivered, curling up into a ball and trying to keep myself warm. I couldn't help but think of Kevin, even sitting trapped in this concrete box, tied to pipe. I still felt terrible for breaking up with him. I knew I was his mistress, but when I was with him, I felt as if I were free. He looked at me every day with no judgement. I knew he adored me, and I knew I had broken his heart, and I just sat there wondering what he was doing right now. I missed him!

Over the next few hours, I reminisced about the times I had with him, how he would touch me, how he looked at me every day, how he knew from the first moment he first touched me that he knew exactly how to satisfy me every single time! I could never work out how he was so in tune with my body and my mind. When he would touch me, it felt as if we both became one. Kevin was a true romantic. I had never been with or experienced a man like him in my life. I loved it when we would just lie on the grass looking into each other's eyes as he would softly run his fingers through mine and play with the tips of my fingers. I knew I was reliving these moments in my head repeatedly to try relax my mind and to distract me from the obvious situation I was facing. I couldn't help but believe or even hope that Robbie wasn't behind this. I kind of giggled to myself as I thought about him. With his temper, I did believe he was capable of seriously hurting me, but I didn't believe he would be behind a mastermind plan of slowly torturing me, or whatever this was, for that matter.

I could see from the window that it was starting to get gradually darker, and I couldn't believe I was going to be spending another night in a frosty shithole! I had to stay focused and positive if I were to survive, as I still didn't even know why I had been brought here.

I heard a noise that sounded as if a car was slowly driving over crushed rocks. I tried to get up off the floor, but my hands were linked to the pipe and my legs had gone fully numb. I was desperately struggling to try to control them. I used all my strength to get my body off the ground. My legs were shaking, and I had severe pins and needles running through them as I slid my hand around the pipe and slowly pulled my body up to a full standing position. I felt it was the best way I could protect myself from what was about to happen.

I heard a car door slam and then another door sound. I could hear people talking but couldn't work out what they were saying. I heard the door lock sound and could see the door handle slightly moving as someone was trying to unlock the door of the room I was in. A man I had never seen before entered. He appeared to be in his late sixties and had grey spiky hair. He was wearing jeans and a white and navy blue striped golfer's shirt. He walked over to me and kept coming closer, stopping only a step away from me, very close to my face. "Hi, Ella. How are you today? How's the head feeling?"

I tried to move my legs and get the feelings back in them so I could try to protect myself as he got closer to me. I became nervous, as I wasn't sure what this man was capable of. He lightly started to touch my face with his keys. He ran one key from my forehead to my chin. "Ella, you have no idea who I am, but I certainly know who you are!"

I tried to move my face away from him, but he grabbed my chin tightly and then held my face so I couldn't move it at all. I had no choice but to look at him. I tried to scream, but my screams just were muffled through the cotton rag. He laughed at me, and I could hear the pleasure in his tone. "Are you trying to say something?" he asked as he continued to laugh. He then slightly loosened my gag at the back of my head until it fell to the ground.

"Who are you? What do you want?" I demanded.

"What do I want …? I want a lot of things, Ella!" He started to pinch and move my clothes. "I remember that red number you wore at the ball. God, you looked good!" he said as he got even closer to me.

"Get away from me!" I screamed.

He kept laughing at me, clearly knowing he was in full control and I was trapped in his little game. He stood back and started to unbuckle his belt. He unclipped his top button of his pants and then pulled down his zip. My heart sank. I knew what was about to happen to me, and I was stuck to a pipe. There was nothing I could do! I started to scream out for help at loud as I possibly could. I started thrusting my body all over the place, trying to get him away from me and trying to stop him from touching me.

He grabbed my face and demanded, "Shut up! What are you getting so upset for? I will make sure you enjoy yourself as much as I am about too!"

I spat at his face, hitting him below his eye, and then tried to kick him away from me, stabbing his shins with my heels. He grabbed my dress with one hand and squeezed my chin with his other hand, forcing his body onto mine, pushing me against the pipe. "You are a disgusting pig! Ladies don't behave like that!" he said, wiping away my saliva from below his eye. "I like fighters; it makes it much more enjoyable." He put his hands up my dress and ripped my stockings right off my body. He then grabbed hold of the band at the top of my underwear and ripped them completely off my body.

I started to beg and plead with him to stop. I was moving my body all over the place and trying to get him leave me alone, but he didn't care! I could tell he got pleasure from it. The more I pleaded with him to stop, the more he got off. He pulled down his pants and moved his hand from my chin to my throat, holding his grip so strongly that I could hardly breathe. He was choking me.

I heard the door sound, and an old woman walked into the room. She could see the man choking me with his pants down and moving my dress, and knew I was only moments away getting raped. "Am I interrupting the two of you? I see you have met! Larry, get your cock back in your pants, please. You will have your chance. Don't worry about that!"

He pulled up his pants and stepped away from me. He went over to the woman and said, "I'll leave you two alone!" Then he left the room.

The woman came over to me and asked, "Are you hungry? You must be hungry by now, Ella."

I ignored the question and demanded her to tell me what was going on.

"Well, I don't care if you're hungry anyway. Sorry, no oat smoothies for you today!" she said, breaking into laughter.

"So that's what this is about!" I said.

"You have no idea how many people you have pissed off with your little games, Ella!"

The man returned with a plate of food and put it on the floor in front of me, telling me to eat something, as I was going be there for a while and he wanted me to have full strength for when he was ready for me.

I told them both, "Unless one of you intends on feeding me, my hands are tied to this pipe so I won't be able to feed myself."

With a filthy look on her face, the woman said, "You're a whore. I'm sure you'll feel right at home on your knees!"

The man approached me with a Stanley knife and put it up to my throat, then slowly moved it to the back of my hands and cut away at the cable tie that was tied to the pipe. My hands were still tightly tied behind my back. He said to her, "If she's that hungry, she will work it out. Let's go!" The man walked over to me and then pushed me into the corner of the two walls, grabbing my hair pulling me up as he put his hand around my throat to chook me. He then put his hand straight up my dress and slid his fingers inside me. I froze. "We'll have our fun later. I will be back to finish what we started!" He took his fingers out of me, and then they both walked out of room and locked the door behind them.

As soon as they left, I felt a sudden rush of adrenaline hit me. I had to escape. My wrists were facing each other behind my back, and I knew I had to change that if I were to get out of here. I tried to wriggle them both to face outwards, but the cable tie was cutting deep into my skin. *I have to fight*, I thought. *I have never been a quitter, and I'm not going to start today.* If I was going to survive, I knew I was going to have to inflict a lot of pain on myself to do so.

I slowly started to wriggle one wrist at a time. The cable tie was cutting into my skin, and it was bleeding a lot, but it was working, so I had to persevere and keep going! I managed to get one wrist around, so I started to work on the next. I could feel the blood tickle my skin as it slowly ran down my hands from my wrists and then dripped from my fingertips onto the cold concrete floor. I finally got the other wrist around. I took a deep breath and quickly lifted my arms over my head. I could tell straight away that my plan was not going to work. The pain of that positon was far too much, and I was going to dislocate something in the process. I got down into a squatting position and tried to push my hands against my lower back to my bum, trying to push one leg through my hands. It took a lot of wiggling and rolling around, but I did it. I started with the other leg. I got my foot through and then slowly pushed my knee through until both legs were free. I cried aloud in pain. I had made it. It was so painful, but my hands were free and now resting in front of me.

I went straight up to the window and tried to see out the window, but I wasn't tall enough, and there was nothing else in the room that I could use to gain the height I required. I went to the door and tried to open it, which seemed like a silly thing to do, as I heard and watched them lock it, but it was worth a try! What else did I have to lose by doing so? I walked back over to where I had been tied up to the pipe and decided to have something to eat, as I was beyond starving. I got down on the ground on both of my bare knees. The floor was rough and cold, and my flesh was directly on the concrete surface, as that creep had ripped my stockings off earlier. I moved both hands towards the plate and used my right hand to pick up food. It was only a packet of instant rice that hadn't been microwaved, but I was so hungry that I didn't care.

I crawled into the corner shaking, as I was beyond cold at this point. I was freezing! I sat there for hours and kept stewing on the incident earlier. The man had brought back memories I had buried a long time ago, but I couldn't shake the feeling. I felt as if I were ten years old again and … helpless. I kept visualizing being strangled and coming in and out of consciousness. I tried my hardest to shake the feeling I had. I tried desperately to think of my happy place. *Where is my happy place …? Kevin.* I felt as if those memories of Kevin were going to be the only thing to keep me alive.

Somehow, after the day I had, I managed to fall asleep. I woke to the light shining into the room from the window. I slowly stood up and started to walk around the room to stretch my legs. The cramps were borderline worse than the previous day. I slowly started to walk around the room, bending my knees as I went along. I kept trying to figure out who the old couple were and why the hell I was locked in a concrete box. I mean, this stuff only ever happened to me for some reason. I had always attracted crazies. I had been stalked and followed in the past, but kidnapped … Well, this one topped it. I couldn't work out what kind of woman could see another woman almost be assaulted and not even bat an eyelid. I felt she was far more evil than he was, to allow something as crude as that to happen. She clearly had much hatred for me and didn't care what was to happen to me. The more I thought about it, the more I couldn't help but try to find the link between my kidnappers and Kevin. Only Kevin drank that particular drink! My heart started to race. I hoped Kevin hadn't put me in this positon! Surely he wouldn't let someone hurt me. It didn't make any sense. He couldn't handle watching me dance with my girlfriends as random men on the dance floor tried to grind on me, and now he was allowing someone to rape me.

As my heart continued to race and my hands shook with the sickening thought, I continued to pace around the room. I noticed two metal bars over the window. I went over to the window. It was around half a metre taller than my head, and I decided to try to jump to reach the bars. The more my brain thought about the slight chance that Kevin had something to do with this, the more I felt sick to my stomach. I was determined to get out of here. I needed to get an idea of where I was! I tried to jump as high as I possibly could to reach to grab the bars, but I wasn't tall enough, and it made it extremely hard for me, as my hands were still tied together, but I kept trying until I slipped and fell to the ground, hitting my side and grazing the side of my thigh on the concrete, which had cut open the skin on my elbow. My body was so cold, and I could feel that I had hurt myself, but I didn't know the full extent, for my body had gone partially numb. I sat there for a minute, trying to work out how to get up there. I needed to see what was outside. I decided to try one more thing.

I walked to the opposite wall to the window, took a deep breath, and started to run towards the wall. As I got close to the wall, I bent my knees and jumped as high as I could towards the wall. I used the grates in my shoes on the wall to try to get traction and then quickly reached my hands up to try to grip one of the bars. I just managed to grip the bar, but I was weak and kept losing my grip. I held on for a minute and tried to pull myself up even the tiniest bit to get a glimpse out of the window. I did have strong arms from all of the yoga and pilates I did almost every day. I was conditioned to holding my own body weight, but I was still struggling. I managed to pull myself up just enough to see outside. All I could see were dried paddocks of yellow grass and a grey gravel driveway. The driveway dropped off onto a hill, so I couldn't see the end of the driveway. I couldn't see any animals or people, and there were no close neighbours I could see. I let go of the bar and walked back over to the corner. Sitting down on the ground, hugging my knees into me chest, I tried to figure out where I was, feeling defeated, as I had hoped I would have a better understanding of what was going on.

Kevin received a phone call at nine the next morning from Kim, letting him know that she had thought about what he said and was not signing anything until next week, as she had an appointment with her family's lawyer. She told him that she had a couple things she had to do and that she wasn't going to be making any further decisions until then. Kevin seemed disappointed but had no choice but to accept her terms.

I had been sitting there for hours in the silent icebox when I heard a car coming back up the driveway. It came to a complete stop. I heard three car doors sound this time. I was scared, for I didn't know what was going to happen this time or who the other person was! I heard them at the door, trying to unlock and open it. The old man and woman walked back into the room. "Hello again! Did we have a comfortable sleep last night, sweet pea?" the old woman said as she laughed uncontrollably.

The man left me alone with the old woman again. She just stood there snarling at me until the man returned with another plate of rice. He walked over to me and then leaned down and placed the plate on the ground next to where I was standing. He came back up to full stance and stepped closer to me. I kept walking backwards, trying to get away from him. I walked myself into his trap, directly in the corner. I had nowhere to go. He leaned his body against mine and put his hand up my dress, running his fingers up my inner thighs and then slowly making his way up to my private area, running his fingers back and forth, until he put one finger inside me. I shouted at him to stop and tried with all my force to push him off me, but he was far too strong.

I looked over at the old woman and started yelling at her in a panic. "What's wrong with you? How can watch him do this to me!" She sniggered at me and just continued to watch me. She pulled a knife out of her bag and pointed in my direction as he unzipped his pants. They say that when certain situations arise in life, we take flight or we fight. In this moment, I believe I did both. A part of me refused to beg or plead this time, as I knew that they both would get pleasure from it. I refused to give them that satisfaction, even though my heart was racing and all I wanted to do was kick, punch, and scream. I remained calm and didn't fight him. I also knew that they were going to try to kill me, and as I was well outnumbered, I was still unaware of who the other person was. I had to preserve as much energy as I possibly could for that fight.

He put himself inside me, to my disgust, and started to thrust his body against mine. I kept eye contact with the sadistic bitch the entire time. I looked into her eyes, but I didn't think anything. My mind went blank. It had to block what was happening right in this moment, so my mind just shut down. I could automatically tell that neither of them was keen about how calm I was, considering the situation. He was holding my hands above my head with both of his hands when he suddenly released one of his hands and punched me with his free hand. I took two blows to the face, the second blow causing my lip to split. My head pushed backwards, hitting the wall behind me, and I still gave no reaction. I pretended it didn't hurt, even though it did, but I had so much adrenaline pumping through my system that the pain was minimal. Each breath I took, I could feel the warm air on my exhale hitting my cracked lip and stinging. The man was brutal and got off every time he inflicted pain on me. I knew the fight for my life was coming closer, but I also knew that there was a strong chance I was going to die today, and if that was the case, I was going to die on my terms and no one else's!

He punched me in the stomach, then in the face again. Still I didn't react. He then asked the woman to pass him the knife and held it right up against my throat. My heart rate dramatically increased, and I honestly thought my heart was going to burst right out of my chest. I was thinking that this was it. My life was finally over! He started yelling at me. "Come on, Ella … Look me in the eyes, you fucking whore, or I'll slice your throat!" He said this with venom in his tone as he grabbed my jaw with force and pulled my face in his direction, holding it there and squeezing it tightly in his grip until I made complete eye contact with him. He then scraped the knife down my throat, slightly grazing the skin and drawing blood.

As I felt the blood lightly run down the front of my neck, I knew, or had a feeling, that he wouldn't kill me in this position until he had satisfied himself. I kept telling myself to go to my happy place and remain calm, even in the position I found myself facing. I was always overthinking things, rationalising a situation. My mind was always going crazy. I kept saying to myself, *They can have my body. It's just a body, but I refuse to give them my soul, and I would rather die than let them break me. They cannot break me.*

The man was becoming extremely frustrated, and his thrusts became harder and deeper as he placed his hand around my throat, choking me with one hand and still holding the knife in the other. His thrusts lessened until he became completely limp. He stopped and then took himself out of me, removing his hands from my body and taking the slightest step back. He was still standing extremely close to me. My heart was racing, and I wasn't sure if I had made my situation worse, as he was extremely pissed off that he didn't get to finish!

He took a step back again and looked over at the woman, holding the knife in his left hand, and then looked back at me and smiled as he raised his right hand and punched me one more time, hitting me in my nose this time. I just stood there in the corner with my hands resting in front of me. "You know, Ella, if you had just stayed away from him, you wouldn't be in this predicament! I can see why Kevin couldn't help himself; I really don't blame him. I couldn't help myself either!" He sniggered as he did up the top button of his jeans.

The woman interjected, saying, "Kevin has always had a thing for blonde whores. So has my husband.' She rolled her eyes. "You see, Ella, we have to do what's best for everyone! It's bigger than just you and him. So I made a deal with my husband. I get what I want, and he gets what he wants. Win-win for both!"

I heard someone knock at the door, and the woman yelled out to the person to come in. The door opened, and *that* person walked in behind them. I took one look at her and recognised her face instantly. I knew this person. She looked at the man and said, "I am guessing you have finished?" He nodded, and she laughed and then walked towards me.

"Hi, Kim," I said.

"Are you surprised, Ella?" asked Kim, as a look of delight appeared on her face.

"Not really. I'm guessing this is your disgusting piece of shit father and your evil bitch of a mother!" I said in disgust.

"You're going to make it so easy for me to get rid of you with that attitude!" said Kim, snarling at me.

"We are not only doing this for our daughter; we are doing it for Kevin's sake as well!" said Kim's father.

"The greater good," said her mother.

"I could tell at the ball that you were dangerous, but I didn't expect it to get this far!" he said. "As the months rolled on, we all watched with concern."

"Why?"

"He has never brought any of his toys to his charity ball!" said Kim's father. "That stood out; it was the first sign of what was to come. Then Kevin started cancelling meetings and rarely actually worked, when he had previously poured his heart and soul into his family's company."

I was so shocked, and I replied, mocking them, "So that's why you kidnapped me—because Kevin brings a date to his charity function that your daughter, his wife, had no intension of showing up for. And because he isn't showing up to meetings! You kidnapped me and sexually assaulted me, and now you are going to kill me because Kevin isn't showing up for meetings. Are you fucking serious?" I asked them sarcastically, in utter shock. I was so disappointed and angry! I truly believed my life was worth more than that.

Kim replied, shaking her head, "Who really cares about his stupid charity function? My God, get over it! She died, like, thirty years ago. And *no!* It's because he's in love with you! Did you know that the prick served me with divorce papers three days ago over breakfast? *It's all your fault!* Why did you have to sleep with him?" She started to scream at me as her anger levels dramatically increased.

"I am not the first woman you know that he has cheated on you with!" I said.

"Yes, I am well aware of the life my husband leads! Kevin always gets whatever Kevin wants. But we had a good thing going on, you know. I have my life, and he has his! And I get to spend his money! You know, he only wants to pay me out twenty million dollars. What a fucking joke!" Her anger increased to a whole other level. "Why did you have to fuck him!" she asked me as she became increasingly unstable while questioning me. "Why?"

Why did I fuck your husband …? Let's see … I don't know! I don't know why you don't! He's really good in bed, you know. Ah, wait. That's right. He can't stand your cold bony body—that's why!" I laughed at her.

At this point, I was well outnumbered. I was rather sure I wasn't going to make it out of here alive, so I didn't care. If I was going out, I was going out in style. These were my terms, and I was going to make sure she felt as insecure as possible.

Kim launched herself across the room and started choking me, swinging my head back and forth. She grabbed my face and pushed it up against the concrete wall. She laughed in my ear and whispered, "I'm going to take the pretty look off your face for good, and no one will want you once I am done with you!" She pushed my face and started rubbing it into the wall. I could feel the skin on my face tearing from the grits in the concrete. I know that what she was doing was bad, but I refused to let her know she was hurting me. I refused to give her any sense of pleasure from my pain. She pushed me with force and dragged my face across the wall.

Out of nowhere, her father grabbed her by the wrists, pulling her backwards away from me. "Not yet, Kim! Not Yet. We had a deal; I want her alive!" he told her as he dragged her off me kicking and screaming.

Her mother stood back and watched in disgust, saying, "Not long for this world, my dear! Not long at all!"

The old man grabbed them both by the arms and dragged them out of the room. I heard their car doors slam and the vehicle start and then drive away back over the rocks. My body just collapsed and fell to the floor. I sat there for a moment thinking and then crawled into the corner of the room, hugging and squeezing my body tightly into my legs and chest, trying to stay warm and comfort myself. My body felt battered and bruised. I lightly touched my face with my fingertips. It felt as if I'd been burnt with a blowtorch. As much as my face hurt, I wasn't too worried. I guess I was vain, but I was going to supposedly die in the next few days, so what did it matter what I looked like anymore! As I sat there, I couldn't help but feel some sense of relief that Kevin wasn't involved whatsoever. I thought about both of the men in my life, and I wondered if anyone was even out searching for me yet or if they had concluded that I had just run away.

I decided to eat the rice they had brought me. It was terrible and plain, but after all, it was my last supper, you could call it, if Kim got her way, and I was absolutely starving as well. I had been famished the entire time, but I think the stress of the situation kept putting it out of my mind. I wasn't sure why they didn't just kill me two days ago! What were they waiting for? I could tell Kim was disgusted by her father's actions, and I believe she pretended to proudly laugh, when really she was ashamed! But I felt she wanted me to suffer so badly because she had so much hatred built up for me, which is why she allowed her father to do what he did—to get back at me!

I leaned the back of my head against the wall until I fell asleep in the same place, my head slouched and hair resting on the same wall, as I did the night before, shivering in the corner of two concrete walls.

CHAPTER 16

My Fight

A DAY LATER, I woke up to a car speeding up the driveway. I opened my eyes and could see the room fully lit from the sun. I had slept in longer today than I had the days before. It was probably because I felt as if a truck had hit me. I got up off the ground as quickly as my legs would allow me to. I listened but heard only one door sound. I waited but didn't hear another. I could hear someone urgently trying to get into the room. I wanted so badly to believe that this could be someone who had realised that I was missing and had been held here, that this person had come to rescue me! But this was no fairy tale. My worst fear was that it was Kim's father, here to get what he wanted and then finish me off for good this time! Someone was trying to unlock the door but struggling. I think that was because the person was in a mad rush.

The door flew open with force, and it surprised me to see that it was Kim. She launched herself across the room at me, pushing me up against the corner wall, hitting my face, and choking me. I put my hands up to try to protect my face, while she was frantically yelling at me, "How could you! How could you? I have to kill you now! I can't go on waiting any longer!" I was struggling to try to stop her from hitting me and scratching open my facial wounds. I kicked her left knee, and she fell backwards on to the floor. I jumped straight on top her and started strangling her with my cable tie handcuffs. I had my wrists tilted at an angle, holding the cable ties right up against her throat so she couldn't breathe! She was trying so hard to fight back, but I was much stronger than she was. Even in my weak condition and with all her rage, I still had more strength then she did. After all, she was all bones. She reached out her left arm and grabbed the plate on the ground, hitting it over my head. The plate smashed, and the pieces fall to the ground. As the plate hit my head, I accidently loosened my grip around her throat. I lost enough grip, and she managed to get some air, saying in a broken voice, "You're pregnant by him!"

I immediately tightened my grip and watched as the tears from the struggle ran away from her eyes. I pushed my wrists into her throat even harder, twisted my hand as I was squeezing my wrists down harder. I leaned my body weight on my elbow and held her. I then slowly picked up a piece of the broken plate from the ground with my other hand. I pushed the sharp, narrow piece up against her, piecing the skin on her throat with it. I then pushed it in even further and watched the blood instantly flow out and around the piece of ceramic and down the side of her neck. I whispered into her ear, "I was."

I stood up and leaned my back against the wall, watching her until I saw her take her last and final breath. I then went back to the floor, got down on to my knees, and grabbed another piece of the broken plate, trying to frantically free my hands, using it as if it were a knife. It wasn't working. I didn't know how long I had until the others came back, but I knew I didn't have long and needed to leave immediately. My fight instincts had just kicked in, and I saw the keys on the floor, which Kim had dropped in the struggle. I picked them up and ran out of the room, making my way out of the house.

It was the first time in four days since I had been outside. I ran for her car, squinting from the blurring sun and trying to unlock her car, urgently pushing the button down continuously. I had to use both my hands to pull the door handle up to open the door. I got into Kim's red Mercedes and started the engine. I had to push the button and the brake at the same time to get the car to start. I pushed down the lock button on the right-hand side of the door, took the car out of park, and then put it into drive. Using both hands, I pushed in the button and pulled the handbrake off lock, putting my foot on the accelerator and starting to drive down the driveway. I found it hard to steer, as my hands were still tied together. I had so much adrenaline pumping through my body. I had just killed Kim and escaped from my concrete icebox prison.

When I got to the end of the long driveway, I turned left and followed the road until I got to the end. I turned left again, but this time onto a main road I continued to drive until I reached a town. I was driving for several minutes when I saw a sign in the distance on the left-hand side of the road. As I got closer, I could see that it stated that the next town was only three kilometres away.

Minutes later, I drove into the town. The main street was lined in jacaranda trees and historical building with cute country-style shopfronts. I could see a fire station up ahead in the distance, with a fire truck and men in uniform standing out front. I drove straight towards the station and pulled into the driveway, only stopping moments before hitting one of the men. I pulled up the handbrake and urgently tried to get out of the car as I was screaming for help and crying. I fell out of the car in my distressed panic, and the firemen rushed over to my aid. "Help me! They're going to kill me!" I ranted, pleading them for their help. One of the men picked me up off the ground, and another threw a blanket around me. He carried me over to the garden retaining wall next to the shed and placed me down, wrapping me in the blanket. The man kneeled down to check that I was okay and asked me for my name. I told him, "My name is Ella … Ella Jade Moore," I replied as I just sat there spent and looking down at him.

"Nice to meet you, Ella! Those cable ties look very uncomfortable. Let me fix that for you," he said as he reached into his pocket and pulled out a Swiss Army knife. It was much larger than a normal pocketknife and had a sharp unusual-looking rippled blade. I put my arms out in front of me as he started to gently cut the cable ties off my bruised and bloodied wrists. He tried his best to relax my hands and tried comforting me, as my hands were shaking uncontrollably. He held on to my dried and bloodied hands gently and kept reassuring me, telling me, "It's all going to be okay. You are safe now! I promise you, Ella, that no one can hurt you now!"

He placed the knife down and told me the police were on their way. Then he passed me a glass of water. I was so thirsty and jittery that I couldn't even drink from the glass properly. I was spilling it down the front of me, and it was dripping down my chin. It was so embarrassing. I tried to take the lightest of sips. I heard one of the men whisper to the other, "That's the missing woman from the news. I'm sure of it!"

As I slowly sipped the water, a police car arrived. Two gentlemen got out of the police car and walked directly over to me, holding their notepads and pens. The first police officer introduced himself and the other officer. He then asked me a few questions, asking if I was okay, how I was feeling, and inquiring about my name and age.

I replied, "My name is Ella Jade Moore. I'm thirty-two years old, and I am so cold and sore; I cannot stop my body from shaking!"

"I am so sorry to cut you off there," he said to me. He looked straight at the other officer and said, "This is the woman that has been missing for the past four days. We have to call this in!" The officers apologised to me and said they would be back shortly. They had to make a few phones calls.

One of the firefighters walked over to me while I was waiting. He passed me a drink and told me, "It's a hot chocolate. I don't know if you like them, but you look so cold that I thought it might help you warm up."

I thanked him for his kindness and took the drink from him, starting to sip it. It was so warm and smooth. I normally didn't drink milk, but I was so hungry, thirsty, and cold that I didn't care. I could have ingested anything warm at this point! The hot chocolate was sweet, creamy, and delicious. I don't think I had ever tasted something so scrumptious in my life to date. Being deprived for days made it taste so much more enjoyable than it probably was.

I had been waiting awhile when another police car pulled in. It flew in the driveway and came to a sudden stop. A man got out the car and rushed over to me with his mobile phone, instantly getting down on his knees to meet my face height. "Ella, I am so glad to see you! You don't know who I am, but I've been trying to find you since you disappeared four days ago. My name is Detective Sergeant Andersen." I was lightly running my fingers over my cut wrists and bruises as I was listening to him speak. He put his hand gently over the top of my hand and said, "We will get you cleaned up, and then, if you are up to it, I would like—while it is still fresh on your mind—for you to tell me what has happened to you and where you have been for the past four days. I'll let you finish your hot drink first. You look as if you're freezing." He started to come to full stance.

I nodded in agreement and grabbed his hand. "Wait! Kim Jacobs is dead. I had no choice; she was going to kill me! I had to protect myself. You have to believe me!" I said frantically. "There were two others, but they weren't there when it happened—but they will come back! I know they'll come back."

He asked me, "Would you be able to remember how to get to the place you were held?"

I told him, "I'll try, Sergeant Andersen, but I can't promise you anything! It all happened so quickly, and I just wanted to get out of there. The whole thing feels like a blur!"

He took my hand and said, "Let's go for a drive, Ella, and there's no harm if you cannot remember. I promise you I will catch them!" I stood up and made my way slowly, walking over to his car. He went around to the passenger side of the car and opened the door for me. After he waited for me to gently get in and sit down, he then closed my door as he walked around the car to the driver's seat. He yelled out to the other officers, who were leaning up against their car, and told them to request backup, saying that they needed to follow him, as there may be others and he was not sure if they were armed or not.

He went to open the driver's side door and said, "Wait! Can you also call for a coroner? I have a feeling one will be required!"

"Yes, sir," they responded. They both got into their vehicle, following right behind him.

Sergeant Andersen got into the car, and started the engine. He took the handbrake off and then put the car into reverse. He reversed out, making a backwards U-turn to straighten up the vehicle. He then turned the heater up nice and high for me, and I laid the blanket over my cut and bruised exposed legs. I was cold, but I was also embarrassed. I felt naked and needed to try o cover my ripped clothes. "Which way?" he asked me, looking left and then right. I told him to turn left and follow the road.

We were in the middle of nowhere. There were many ld farms on large acreage properties on a narrow highway. There were heaps of narrow dirt tracks off the highway and nimal warning signs; everything looked the same. We had been driving for around twenty minutes when I asked him to pull over, as I felt flustered and lost. I couldn't remember which rack I had come out from. I asked him if he could turn around nd slowly drive back in the other direction, as it would help og my memory, for I had originally come from that direction. He nodded his agreement, putting his indicator on and slowly ulling onto the rocks on the left side of the road. He then made right-hand turn to go back in the direction we had just come rom. We had been driving in the other direction for around ight minutes when I told him I remembered the trees and the ign, adding that it must have been the last road we had just riven past. He patiently indicated to the left again and slowly ulled off the road, making a right-hand turn. He slowly drove ack in that direction for a minute, until I told him to stop. This one—turn right," I insisted. He turned right, and the olice car behind us continued to follow in the same direction.

We were driving up the old road for a couple minutes when saw a white painted hardwood fence with farm gates in the istance. I asked him to slow down. I'd sped out of there so uickly while escaping that I really wasn't taking much notice, ut the fence did look familiar to me! I told him I wasn't sure ut asked him if we could try this one. He pulled into the riveway with the white gates, as I had requested, and as we ot closer, my anxiety started to increase. I began to sweat and alk aloud to myself, saying, "Deep breath!" I kept telling myself hat repeatedly, trying to calm myself down as we got even loser. We drove up the driveway until we reached the massive farmstead horse ranch at the top of the hill. I imagined that this house had been designed for the wealthy horse-loving family. I told him, "This was it! This is where I have been locked up for the past days!" I felt sick to my stomach being back in this place. Sergeant Andersen stressed to me that I was safe with him and he was going to wait for backup before any of them made a move, as he was not leaving me alone. He played around with his multimedia screen in his car, tapping into different screens on the touch screen, until he got to his contacts screen. He then made a phone call, letting them know the exact address of our location.

We waited for about fifteen minutes, and then three cars pulled in behind us. All the men jumped out with their guns drawn and walked over to the vehicle I was sitting in. Sergeant Andersen got out of his car and asked three of the men to stay with his car, explaining that I was the victim and that I was inside the car, saying that under no circumstances were they to let anyone near me or the vehicle. Sergeant Andersen and the rest of the officers followed him into the house, and they all drew their weapons as they rushed in pack form into the house. He reiterated to them not to touch anything as they walked through the door, as it was a crime scene. The door was still open from when I had run out of it earlier. A moment later, I heard them yell, "Clear!"

I'd been waiting in the car for a good five minutes when Sergeant Andersen returned. He told me that they had found where I had been held and that they had found Kim's remains, saying that there was no sign of anyone else in the house. I explained to him, "When I was held there, the others didn't come until it was almost dark. I would watch the window, as it was the only way I could tell the time. I would watch the sunlight shine through the window. It was the only sense of the date and time I had." He told me he was going to take me back to the station and then he could take my statement if I was still up for it. I agreed and told him, "I'd rather get it out of the way, over and done with. "I'm dying to have a shower, put clean warm clothes on, and eat a massive plate of veggies and then some chocolate, maybe even a vegetarian lasagne." I laughed nervously.

As we drove back to the station and returned to civilisation, he informed me that he found my pregnancy test and he had to inform both men, as they were both high suspects in my disappearance. He needed to see both of their reactions to determine if they had any involvement.

"I was aware they must have been informed," I replied. "I'm not sure what Kim's plans were for me, but they got derailed when she found out I was pregnant because she attacked me for the final time alone and didn't have her backup to hold me down as she had previously!"

He told me he needed to inform both men of my return, as he had promised both of them that the moment I was found, he would contact them to let them know, as long as I was happy with his doing so. He asked me who I would like to meet me at the station and pick me up to take me home.

"Could you please call Allan Phillips? He's my stepfather, and I would prefer to go back to his house for the moment! A lot has happened, and I feel very unsure right now. I would just like to be with him!"

Sergeant Andersen asked me with surprise, "Do you mean Sergeant Allan Phillips?"

"Yes," I responded, looking at him curiously, wondering how he knew who my stepfather was.

"Wow, small world! Would you believe he was my very first supervising officer I had when I first joined the force? I'll just make that phone call for you." He gave me a smile and a wink.

When we arrived back at the station an hour later, I could already see Allan was there waiting for me out in front of the station. After the car pulled into the car park, I got out of the car and wrapped the blanket around my body. Allan rushed over to me. He held one hand on his heart and smiled at me, letting out a sigh of relief. He took his hand from his chest and then placed his hands on my head, resting them on my lower cheeks, underneath my wounds, kissing my forehead. He wrapped his arms around my body and began to tightly cuddle me, rocking me side to side. "I am so glad you're okay, kid. I was so worried about you, El. I love you so much!" He grabbed my hand and held it as we walked into the station.

Sergeant Andersen told Allan he needed to take my statement in private and then shook his hand, telling him that he had always looked up to him as an officer. He reassured him that he would look after me. I followed him into the room, and he closed the door behind me. I sat down at the table, leaving space between myself and the table, and then rested my hands on my lap. As time went on, I nervously began to fidget with my fingers underneath the table. Sergeant Andersen said, "Start at the beginning, from Olive Grove Mall. What happened, Ella?" He put a voice recorder on the table.

"I had stopped at the mall to get bits and pieces" Andersen stopped me and told me I had to be more specific. I started again. "I had stopped at Olive Grove Mall for bits and pieces for Robbie's lunch after I finished work for the day. After I did the shopping, I walked out to my car with my groceries. It was very dark, and I thought I heard something, but when I looked around, I couldn't see anything and thought it may have been the rain. I then heard footsteps behind me. When I went to look around, I was struck, and then I was dragged away, coming in and out of consciousness. They threw me into the boot of a car, and everything went black. I woke up the next day in a concrete room with one tiny window, and my head was pulsating; I knew I had been hit in the head with something. I explained to him in detail what I had endured for the past four days, how I had incurred every injury, including how and why I had chunks of flesh taken out of my face. I told him that my stockings and underwear had been ripped off by Kim's father during the incident of the sexual assault and added that he and his wife watched and enjoyed seeing me suffer. I explained to him how I killed Kim in self-defence with the broken ceramic plate that she had smashed over my head. Then I told him about my escape and said that I made my way to the firehouse and reached safety. "Not long after that, I met you!"

Sergeant Andersen thanked me for my statement and told me I needed to go to hospital to be looked over, adding that I was also required to do a rape kit. He then turned off the voice recorder. We both heard a knock at the door, and Andersen called out for the person to come in. The officer told him that he needed to speak with him in private about what had just happened. He asked me if I could remain seated until he knew exactly what was going on, saying that he would be back in a moment. I had only been sitting there for about three minutes when he walked back into the room and shut the door behind him. He showed me and photo and asked me if the people in the photo were the people who had kidnapped me and held me captive.

I replied, "Yes, that's them. Those are Kim's parents!"

He sat down and told me, "That officer just informed me that after we left the house you were held captive in, Kim's parents, Mr. and Mrs. Lawrence, arrived back at the house, obviously for their daily visit, where they were informed by my officers that Kim was dead, that she had died in the struggle, and that you had escaped and were in custody. I was told that Mrs. Ann Lawrence became outraged and lost full control. She drew a weapon on the police officers at the scene. The men tried to get the woman to disarm, but she refused and pulled the gun on the officers. When she went to pull the trigger, she was gunned down in the scuffle."

I sat there in shock. "What happened to Mr. Lawrence?" I asked.

"He is under arrest and on his way down to the station as we speak to be officially charged with kidnapping, assault, sexual assault, and assault on police. He will be locked up for a very long time." He told me that we needed to go to the hospital to be assessed and do the rape kit, as he had mentioned earlier. As soon as that was done, I was free to go home.

Sergeant Andersen walked me out the back door of the police station and then took me off to the hospital, which was only minutes down the road, to be assessed. After I had been swabbed and checked over by the doctor and nurse, I had wound patches placed on my face. Then I was cleared to go home. Sergeant Andersen took me back to the police station, where my stepfather was waiting for me. He thanked me for my statement and my strength and then told me, "Have a nice long shower or bath and try to warm those freezing bones of yours." He gave me a giant hug goodbye and told me that they had caught the bad guys and I was now safe. I thanked him for treating me with such respect and for not giving up on me and helping me go home.

We walked from the back of the building to the main desk area, and Allan was standing there waiting for me. I told him that we had finished and we were free and now able to go home. I told him I wanted to go back to his house until I sorted things out. He agreed, saying that that was for the best. Allan was an incredible man. He knew exactly what had gone on with Kevin and still held no judgement towards me. He was happy for me to go home with him and still treated me with dignity.

As Allan and I walked out of the police station, I could see a lot people and police officers standing out the front. There was a high traffic of police; I figured they had just arrived back to the station after the shooting and the arrest of Mr. and Mrs. Lawrence. Through the crowd of people, I could see Robbie walking towards me, and then I got a glimpse of Kevin. He was standing in the distance, behind all the people, waiting for me.

As Robbie got closer to me, he seemed happier with every step he took. He rushed over to me and gave me a giant hug. He held me for a moment and then moved his head and whispered into my ear with spitting rage, "You're going to die, you cheating bitch! Is it mine or his! I bet you don't even fucking know, you slut!" I could feel his saliva hitting the side of my face as his temperament changed. He pulled away from me, and then my body was pushed up against his. I felt this overwhelming pain to my stomach and moaned out in pain. I looked down and saw a knife lodged in my belly. Then I watched him pull the knife out of my stomach. I looked up into his eyes as I fell to my knees crying out in pain, holding my stomach, where he had just stabbed me. He grabbed me by my hair and held the bloodied knife against my chin, shouting at me, "You're dead, Ella! I'm going to kill you!"

The police officers drew their guns, yelling at him to drop the knife and step away from me. Robbie cried out, "I can't! She has to die. You don't understand … She is evil!" He moved the knife in a motion to slice my throat, and I heard six gunshots fired. As I saw the shots flying through the air in slow motion, I felt myself being dragged backwards for about two metres, away from Robbie, by Allan and three police officers. I watched the knife fall to the ground and then Robbie fell to his knees. He remained in full eye contact with me until he took his last breath, and then his body fell forward and he landed on his face. I looked down, and there was a lot of blood pouring out of my stomach. I started to cry out for help. "My baby! Please help me. You have to save my baby!"

The police officers were holding me in their arms as Kevin ran over and fell to his knees in front of me. He grabbed my hand and held it firmly as the officers were putting pressure on my stomach to try to stop the bleeding. There was so much yelling—"Where's the ambulance?" and "Hold down firmer!"— as everyone was running around in a panic. It felt like a dream watching everyone screaming and running around in slow motion. I looked at Kevin, and he kept holding me, trying to stay strong as he held on to the bottom of my stomach, rubbing it. Kevin and Allan both tried to reassure me that I was fine and that everything would be okay. I begin to feel light-headed. It could have been the shock. The noises in the background gradually faded out, and I started to feel extremely tired. I tried to keep my eyes open and focus on Kevin, but the feeling was too strong and I couldn't feel the pain in my stomach anymore. It felt so good to close my eyes, so I stopped trying to fight it and just let my body go with it.

I woke up feeling groggy, my eyes slowly opening to a bright and glary room. I could only see white! As I looked around the room, all I could hear was beeping and dripping noises in the background. My eyes opened wide, and I could hear a familiar voice. I realised it was Allan, my stepfather, talking. I tried to block all the background noises and focus, to listen to what he was saying and to whom.

"She is strong, Kevin. She will be fine, and I promise you that! This girl is tough." He put one hand on his shoulder and comforted him. "Did Ella ever tell you about how her father died?"

Kevin responded, "Yes, she told me how he killed himself!"

"Yes, well, I was the first officer on the scene that day. In all my years on the job, I have never seen anything like what I did that day! We arrived at the scene of a suicide to see a ten-year-old little girl, who had just witnessed her father throwing himself off the edge of a cliff in front of her, standing there like an adult and comforting her mother and brother. They just cried in her arms. Trust me. She'll be fine, Kevin!"

Kevin peeped a look into the room, leaning his body into the doorway. "She's awake! Quick, Ella is awake!" Kevin rushed to my bedside and leaned over my body, giving me a gentle kiss on my lips. He then took a seat next to the bed.

Allan came over to me and stood next to my bed facing me. He gently placed his hand over mine, leaned over, and kissed my forehead. "You are one lucky girl, Ella! I told you I never trusted that Robbie; he was too quiet and nice!"

"I know," I responded. "What happened to my baby? Is my baby okay?"

Kevin immediately looked straight at the floor with a grim look to his face. I knew instantly what the outcome had been and started to cry. "No, no, no!" I held on to my stomach.

"They tried really hard, Ella. Your wounds were deep and punctured your superior mesenteric artery ... You lost a lot of blood and were in a bad way! So a decision was made: you or the baby. I am so sorry, Ella!" said Allan as he held me and I continued to cry.

Moments later, the doctors came into the room to check on me. They told me I had had life-saving surgery. I had lost an astonishing amount of blood. My body went into shock, and almost died. They told me that I was recovering reasonably well, considering the circumstances, and that I could go home in around a week's time, but it would be strictly bed rest.

After they left the room, I looked over at Kevin, grabbed his hand, and said, "I am so sorry, Kevin. I am so sorry for everything!" My eyes started to glaze over and become watery.

"Shh. It doesn't matter," he calmly whispered to me.

"No, Kevin! I need to say it. I'm sorry for breaking up with you! I am sorry for not telling you I was pregnant. I didn't know what to do. I felt so lost and confused. I am truly sorry about Kim! I hope you can forgive me," I told him in my broken sobbing voice.

"There's nothing to forgive. I love you unconditionally, Ella!" he told me as he leaned over and kissed me gently on my lips, lightly pinching my chin.

"I love you. You do know that!" I told him as I giggled and put my hand on the side of his face and pulled him in for one more—or maybe two more—kisses.

CHAPTER 17

he Ella Jades

EIGHTEEN MONTHS LATER ...

I leaned my body against the balcony edge and looked over, watching the waves crash onto the rocks as the beautiful sun rose over the horizon. I was wearing a nude lace bra and panty set with an open short white silk robe, letting the fresh summer breeze hit my light golden tanned skin, my belly scar exposed, standing with my fabulously rich husband, who absolutely adored me, as he was staring into my eyes and telling me how much he loved me! I couldn't help but smile as he kissed my neck and held me from behind, rocking me side to side and whispering in my ear, "We are finally free."

I thought back to the wild two and half years we have had together and how my game couldn't have played out any better than it did! My father used to tell me as a young girl that greed, jealousy, and underestimating a person could get a man killed. He was most certainly correct! I couldn't help but think of Kim and Robbie in that moment as I remembered my father's words in my head! Kim's greed and jealously got her killed. I laid the foundations and just had to wait for everyone to come to the table and play with me. Kim was a greedy bitch, but she was no murderer. That was her biggest downfall; that's why she needed her mother and father. I knew that if I were in her situation and I was about to lose my cash cow, I would have seen myself as a threat and would have tried to remove the distraction. I knew Kim would come after me. I didn't know when, but I did know she would eventually try to get rid of me for good. She underestimated me! I did know when I originally was hired that Kevin had a thing for me. I would be stupid and lying to say I thought otherwise. But it wasn't until that day in the boardroom that I realised the power I had over him! And then on Kevin's actual birthday, the day we spent at the beach and then in his shower, the way he looked at me and touched me, it had all changed. It wasn't just power I had over him; he was actually madly in love with me and would do anything for me. It was never about his money. I couldn't care less about it! It was more or less about the challenge. The money and sex were a bonus!

When Kim launched at me with such pain and a look of complete devastation in her eyes, I knew that she loved Kevin. He just never loved her in return. As she was dying, I stood there and watched her. I noticed that she had a look in her eyes. It was as if she felt she was dying for a purpose, a reason, and that her rage was because I was having her husband's baby and she believed that it was worth fighting and dying for! I couldn't help myself. As she was dying, I had to tell her I wasn't pregnant. I could see the look in her eyes turn from liberation to fear, and I just stood there smiling, watching the greedy bitch slowly die! Robbie was harder than I thought he would be. He had always been so jealous and controlling over me, and I believe he never loved me. He just used me and believed he owned me. I had to change that!

Life is a funny thing. Sometimes we can see outrageous things happen right before our eyes, but because our minds cannot cope with this information, it naturally blocks the evidence or the event that actually took place because it didn't make any sense to the mind, so it doesn't register it, so our eyes and minds see something that didn't originally occur. That's exactly what happened with Robbie.

When I'd walked out of the police station with Allan, I could see people and police officers standing out front. I could see Robbie walking towards me, and I could see Kevin standing behind the people, waiting for me. As Robbie got closer to me, he did seem happy to see me. He rushed over to me and gave me a giant hug, holding me in his arms for a moment. I knew that as happy as one can look, with the information he had been given over the past days, there could be no reason in the world he could be honestly happy to see me—and alive, for that matter!

He did whisper in my ear, "You're going to die, you cheating bitch!" with rage as he spat his saliva onto my face.

But as he pulled away from hugging me, I whispered into his ear, "Not before you, baby! Then I slid the Swiss Army knife I had taken from the garden of the fire station and slid it into Robbie's hand. Then I pushed myself against the knife, piecing the knife directly into my own stomach. I moaned out in pain, as the knife was lodged into my stomach. He immediately pulled the knife out of my stomach in shock. It was his instant reaction. He was panicked as I fell to the ground crying out in pain. He had only just woken up to me. He grabbed me by my hair and held the bloody knife against my chin. He was so mad that I had won. He had played right into my game. He knew I had outsmarted him this time!

"You're dead, Ella! You're dead!" he shouted at me in a state of rage. The police officers drew their guns, yelling at him to drop the knife. Robbie started to cry, realising in that moment that there were only two ways that this was going to end, either death by police or in handcuffs. The likelihood of handcuffs was slim at this point. He started yelling that I had to die and that I was evil. As he continued to sob, he moved the knife in a motion to slice my throat. When six shots were fired towards Robbie, it all felt like slow motion. I watched his body take every bullet and jolt as they punctured his body. The knife slowly fell through the air and landed on the ground next to him as Robbie fell to his knees from the bullet wounds. We locked eyes until he took his final breath, and then he fell face first to the ground. His game was finally over! My only opportunity had finally arisen, so I took it. I didn't kill Robbie because I was scared of him. I did believe he was quite capable of killing me—don't get me wrong. He was always capable! But that was not the reason. Here it is … The reason I killed my husband was because I refused to go back to that boring fucking life. I couldn't stand to be a housewife for one more minute. I was no fucking Stepford wife!

CHAPTER 18

The Beginning

WITH KIM AND Robbie both dead, I couldn't help but think back to a place and time where this story really started …

My father … This is where my story really began, and my life as I knew it changed forever. He could always see something in me that he didn't see in my brother or mother. My father had a bad drinking problem, and to call it that was an understatement. No one ever knew the severity of my father's abuse, or if they did, they ignored it. He was brutal to my mother. At dinner, if the potatoes were slightly undercooked or even cold in the centre because he had been standing outside too long smoking and his dinner had gone cold in the meantime, he would stand up and smash his plate directly over her head. The food my mother had spent hours cooking that day was scattered across the floor. He then spent the next two hours yelling at her about what a worthless piece of shit she was and then made her clean up the mess. She just took it. She got down on her knees, defeated and broken as she cleaned up the mess he had made in his rage. He then had a shower and went off to bed, acting as if nothing had happened that evening. He had bipolar schizophrenia, and the booze didn't help. He would come home the next day with flowers for my mother, give her a kiss on her lips, and apologise to her, promising it would never happen again. They would then sit out on the front veranda, looking over at the mountains, and talk about each other's days. This happened regularly from the time I was a small child. You become immune to this type of lifestyle! I started to see the patterns in his behaviour; I started to be able sense his moods and could tell bad days before they had even started.

When my grandfather became ill, that was the moment my life as I knew it changed forever! Even in his weak condition, he was still thinking of me. I remembered him telling me that I had to be strong. I promised him I would never forget who I really was, and he told me that the future was mine to determine however I wanted it to be. Only I could change it! After we had returned after dropping our mother off at my grandparents' house and saying our farewells to our grandfather, literally, as soon as we walked through the front door of our family home, my father asked me what we were having for dinner. I was ten years old, my brother was twelve, and I was the one cooking dinner. I had no choice! I looked through the pantry, trying to find something I could cook for dinner. I found some potatoes and carrots in the bottom of the pantry. I started to peel and slice them up. I then put the sliced vegetables in some pots, filled them with water, and turned on the gas on the stovetop to boil. I looked in the fridge and found one piece of steak, deciding I would cook that for him. I also cooked some two-minute noodles for my brother, as I knew he would have whined that there wasn't enough food.

We ate dinner, and then my brother and father watched TV as I cleaned up the dinner dishes. I was so tired. As soon as I finished, I gave my father and brother a kiss on the cheek and put myself to bed. A couple of days went by, and they were pretty much the same. As the female in the house, it was my job to cook and clean for the males.

On the Tuesday I got home from school, my father was an absolute write-off. He was wasted! As soon as I waked into the house, I was overwhelmed with the strong smell of bourbon and cigarettes. I said hello to my father and then put my school bag down. I took my shoes off, placed them on the shoe rack next to the front door, and then went into the kitchen to get myself a glass of water. I stood in the kitchen facing the wall as I drank my water. My father came up right behind me and stood awfully close to me. I could feel his breath on the back of my neck, and I remember the hairs on the back of my neck standing up. He put his arms on my shoulders and asked me how my day was as he breathed heavily into my ear. I put the glass down and told him my day was good. At the same moment, I could feel something firm leaning against my lower back. I just froze! I had no idea what it was.

He snapped! He snatched my glass off the bench and threw it at the fridge. The glass shattered everywhere. He then grabbed my arms and threw me to the kitchen floor. I could see my brother watching in shock and doing nothing to help me. My father sat on top of me and put his hands around my neck, beginning to choke me, and I hit my head on the floor at the same time. The rage on his face was like nothing I had ever seen before. His face turned bright red and puffy; he looked as if he had been holding his breath. He smashed my head onto the floor. His face got redder, his mouth slightly opened, and he started to drool from his mouth. I did not make one single noise the entire time. I tried to take a breath but couldn't get enough air. I started to come in and out of consciousness. I could see him one moment, and then he was gone the next. I woke up hours later in the same position, lying flat on my back on the floor of the kitchen. I slowly started to sit up and then came into full standing. I looked over at the dining room table, and my brother and father were sitting there eating fish and chips for dinner. I believe I must had been passed out for a good two hours that afternoon. The rest of that week, I had to wear a scarf everywhere to hide the marks and bruises on my throat.

The next time he snapped, he stopped choking me, obviously because it left too much evidence behind the previous time. This time he started holding his hands over my mouth instead, holding down firmly until I couldn't breathe, and this continued for the next two weeks. My brother would question me on the way to school the next day, asking me if it really happened or if he was just suffering with nightmares. My brother was weak. I knew he wouldn't be able to cope if he thought his dreams were reality. He was older than I was, but he was naive. We had already grown up seeing far too much, and I couldn't bring myself to tell him the truth, so I lied. I told him they were bad dreams he was having and not to worry about it, saying that they would go away soon.

To this day, I still remember the look in my father's eyes every time he held me down and bashed my head into the floor. I felt that he was so frustrated could not control his rage. I believe he knew how mentally strong I was compared to the others. And he knew I could handle the pain! I have often wondered if he was trying to break me. I refused to cower for him. That's what he wanted, and I refused to give him the satisfaction. I also believe that part of the reason for his frustration was that conflicting pain upon another person aroused him sexually, and he would bash my head onto the floor even harder, trying to get some release instead of sexually assaulting me. I could see the urge on his face, and because I wouldn't cry like my mother, he was unable to stop himself, so he continued until I passed out.

It was two weeks of this daily torture when we received the call from our mother that Friday night to let us know our grandfather had passed away and we had to go to his funeral the following Monday. I felt relieved that my mother was coming home but heartbroken that the only person in this world who made me feel as if I weren't alone was now gone. My grandfather's funeral was the saddest day of my life. I had never loved anyone like that man! But with his death, I felt that I had an inner strength that I didn't have before.

After the service, we went to the pub for a couple of hours for the wake. My father got drunk and pushy towards other people, and my mother suggested that we make our way back home. He agreed, and my mother started to drive us back home. We got just over halfway home, and my mother and brother were hungry. She asked my father if he would mind if she pulled over at the lookout ahead, as she had some food in the boot and could make a couple of sandwiches to tide us over until we got home. We stopped at the next lookout. It was a cliff right on the edge of the ocean. My brother stayed with my mother to help her with lunch and to pinch the food as she made it. I walked over to the edge and watched the waves crash onto the rocks below us. My father staggered over to where I was standing and stood right next to me. "Ella, I just want to say that I am sorry for what I've done to you the past few weeks. I just can't control this feeling I get sometimes, you know. I would never deliberately hurt you! I love you so much. You are my little angel!" He said this in his drunken stumbling state. He put his arms on my back and started to pat me.

I took his hands off my back, put my arms around his waist, and whispered to him, "I'm not." I pushed him with all my strength towards the cliff's edge. His drunken weightless body fell so easily. His deep brown eyes became one with mine. I felt him look into my soul, and for the first time, he could see his own reflection, which terrified him! I could see the fear in his eyes, and I loved every second of it. I stood there and watched my father's limp body fall slowly through the air, almost featherlike, until his body smashed onto the rocks below.

I quickly looked back to the car and saw that my mother was still making lunches for us, facing the boot of the car. I urgently started to scream and point to the cliff's edge, yelling, "He jumped, Mum! Help! Dad has jumped!" My mother started to run towards me. She looked over the edge and put her hands to mouth, looking devastated. Overwhelmed, she fell to her knees and hysterically began to cry. I stood there comforting her as she held on to my legs, and her sobs began to get louder. My brother ran over and fell to my mother, putting his arms around her and crying as well.

As I rubbed my mother's back and listened to her sobs, I thought about how I was ten years old and had just gotten away with murder! I was now thirty-two years old, and I had lived many lives so far. I had been Ms. Ella Jade Jones and Mrs. Ella Jade Moore. I had been abused, kidnapped, sexually assaulted, and made to be a desperate housewife and a mistress, but never had I been a victim. It might seem as if I played the victim card, but I was a fighter and survivor and truly underestimated by all. Life is a choice! We all have the choice to be who we want to be in this life, and as soon as we decide, we can make it happen. I was proud of myself and who I was, and when I looked into the mirror, the monsters were gone. They had all gotten their karma. I had lived this life so many times so far, but this time I chose to do it differently! I made a choice with my father, and I decided when I met Kevin that I would choose who I wanted to be. And that was to be Mrs. Ella Jade Jacobs … I made that happen!

As I ate my breakfast sitting on the balcony in my new multimillion-dollar mansion that I called home, I decided that I really liked my new life. I was drawn to Kevin like a magnet. Was I in love with him? I am not sure about that. I don't really think I am capable of love, but I do know that the man can satisfy me and keep my brain stimulated as no other has ever been able to before! He has no idea that the woman he sleeps next to every night is capable of the things I am. Life is a game. We get what we need! But I made sure I got what I wanted. I'm happy to stick to this life for a while.

ACKNOWLEDGEMENTS

I WOULD LIKE to take this opportunity to express my gratitude to the following people who contributed to the making of this book.

I would first like to give a special thanks to the strongest woman I know, my mother. I would like to thank her for all the late nights, early phone calls, and the endless amount of affection and encouragement she has given me. She has done nothing but support me my entire life. She has shown me the true strength and worth of a woman, which has helped mould me into the person I am today, and I am forever grateful. She said, "Creative write; it will help ease your stress." She has always known what is best!

I thank my Cameron for his constant support, faith, and trust during the challenges we have faced in this life! Through thick and thin, he has stood by me, and I am truly appreciative of all that he has done for me over all the years. I could not have reached my goals without him! I have been blessed with his love, and I am forever his.

Thank you to Rhys, who is not just my brother but also my best friend. I am so grateful for his never-ending support and encouragement. I feel blessed to have shared this journey with him. I thank him for always believing in me.

I thank my grandfather for teaching me to be tough and showing me the true meaning of unconditional love. He will forever be in my heart. *I'll see you on the other side of the stars old man.*

I would like to give a final thanks to all my family and friends who believed in me. And for all those people who didn't, without you I wouldn't be here.

Printed in the United States
By Bookmasters